Novels by Kelly Cheek

All We Hold Dear
Trial by Fire
The Lost Colony
JackSimile and the Phantom Fury
Spirit Breather
The Piper

The SpiritSense Series
In Restless Dreams
First Light
When We Were Gone Astray
Gazing Into the Abyss

The Facebook Trilogy
Profile
Private Messages
Poked

Gazing Into the Abyss

Kelly Cheek

Cover and book design by Kelly Cheek

ISBN: 978-1-7335022-8-3

Printed in the United States of America

He who fights with monsters might take care
lest he thereby become a monster.
And if you gaze for long into an abyss,
the abyss gazes also into you.

Friedrich Nietzsche

1

Waves, a deep purple in the darkening twilight, drifted lazily, endlessly against the shore, sighing over the rocks, then shyly slipping back into the harbor, hidden beneath the next surge.

The moving van had pulled away from the odd-looking house several hours before. Countless boxes had been unloaded and moved in, but not much furniture.

Externally, the house suffered from an identity crisis. The central structure resembled a small Scottish castle, complete with a crenelated battlement and a round turret tower. Through the years, additions had been made, apparently drawing more on styles of the locale or the times, and less on that of the original structure.

Inside, the style was more cohesive, resembling many homes from this area on the North Shore of Massachusetts, but from a couple of centuries earlier. Now, though, the interior was littered with cardboard boxes in nearly every room, adding a modern, if cluttered, look to the house.

"Do you think you have enough books?" Suzy asked as she looked at all the boxes in the space that had been designated Fin's office. She sat on the floor, next to the little dog bed, one of several that were already in several rooms of the house. She was idly petting Ursula, Fin's Pomeranian, who tended to follow Fin around wherever he went.

"To a devoted reader and writer," Fin replied with a mock haughty tone, placing an organizer in the desk drawer, "there's no such thing as 'enough books.'"

"I'm just concerned that the room is too small, now that I see everything in here."

"No, it'll be fine," Fin smiled. "There'll be more room once the books are on the shelves and all the boxes are out of here." He looked around at the room. "And thank you again for letting me have this. I think it'll be perfect. I don't think any sci-fi and fantasy writer could ask for a better studio than the top of a stone turret in a castle."

Suzy had designated the room at the top of the turret on the corner of her house for Fin's office. There were several tall, narrow windows around the turret. Though they were a little wider, they gave the impression of arrow slits in the castle wall.

The bulk of the furniture that Fin had moved from his home in Colorado was for the office, his desk and several cherry bookcases. The bookcases were positioned around the perimeter of the room, between the windows. There was one larger window, facing the harbor, and that's where Fin placed his desk.

"Did you see the look on the movers' faces when I told them all this furniture went at the top of the curved staircase?" Suzy grinned.

"I did," Fin replied. "Poor guys. But the pizzas and cold pop you had waiting for them after the last one seemed to help them get over it."

"Yeah, listen," Suzy said, and Fin immediately recognized the sarcastic tone in her voice, "if you're going to live out here, you need to learn how to talk right. It's soda, not pop."

"Well," Fin intoned, thrusting his chin forward and doing his best Alistair Cooke impression, "we westerners are simply enchanted by onomatopoeia."

"Whatever," Suzy said. Fin couldn't be sure if her response implied that she didn't know what the word meant, or that she felt outdone by his remark. He was okay with either. "Aren't you tired?"

"Exhausted." As he pushed his chair back from the desk, Ursula, recognizing the sound, lifted her head and looked at him. When he stood up, so did she, and she gave her body a shake.

Fin came around the side of his desk and held his hand out to Suzy. She grasped it and he pulled her up, and Suzy grunted as she regained her feet.

"I'm too much of a gentleman to say anything about the 'old noise' you just made," Fin said.

"Shut up," Suzy sniped. "Forty-two isn't old."

"You still look awfully good considering your antiquity," he grinned, and he put his arm around her shoulders. Ursula bounced down the stairs ahead of them as they leaned against each other, heading down to the second floor and the bedroom.

§

Suzy and Fin spent the next few months settling into their new living arrangements. As they both tended to be homebodies, before moving in together, they hadn't been overly affected by self-isolation during COVID's rampage, talking and texting every day, as if they weren't separated by two thousand miles. But now, both fully-vaccinated and healthy, they were happy to actually be together. They got along well, as they had from the start, but they were each plagued with mental torments about their relationship.

Suzy had lost Mark and Emma, her husband and daughter, in a boating accident a few years before. She hadn't planned on allowing anybody else back into her life. But then Fin came along, and Suzy was attracted, despite her best efforts to fend it off. As the attraction turned to love, she still battled guilt, feeling as if she was being unfaithful to Mark with this interloper. But her feelings for the interloper were strong enough that she couldn't send him away.

Ultimately, she undertook an extensive remodeling and redecorating of her house, in an effort to wash away the visual memories of Mark that were loitering there.

Fin had no such ghosts of the past haunting him, unless you counted Mark. Suzy had been in love with her late husband right up to the day he died, and Fin, being a rather insecure type, felt as if her love for Mark was an insurmountable barrier, a goal that he might never attain.

Even though Suzy went to the effort and expense to make her house a welcome place for him, as far as Fin was concerned, Mark was still there, lingering in nearly every room, standing in his way.

Neither of them spoke of their personal romantic demons. Instead, they both focused their attention on their everyday lives with each other. To each of them, it seemed idyllic, despite the apprehensions constantly lingering in their minds.

One of the things that captured their attention was dealing with ghosts. Not the emotional kind that stood in the way of their burgeoning romance, but real spirits of the dead.

Suzy and Fin had met four years before, online, while each doing independent research on a genealogy website. That was at the same time that Suzy discovered the uncanny ability she possessed with relation to the ghost in her carriage house. She was able to communicate with this ghost, make a psychic connection with her, and see her memories, her life, from her perspective, and ultimately helped her to transition to "the other side."

As Suzy explained it, this ability which she referred to as SpiritSense, being able to connect with spirits around them, didn't require any special skills. Rather, it was an innate ability that required only an open mind and some cultivation.

After a while, Fin demonstrated that the cultivation was, apparently, not as much of a prerequisite as the open mind when, to his chagrin, he began to pick up the ability himself.

That ability came to a head before Christmas of that year, after he wrecked his car and ended up in a hospital that just happened to have a ghost. Fin connected with the ghost to such an extent that it rendered him comatose.

It wasn't until Suzy flew to Colorado, leaving her remodeling and redecorating project behind, and made contact with the spirit herself that she was able to break its connection with Fin and help the spirit on to the next plane.

That episode was witnessed by doctors and nurses gathered in Fin's room. To Suzy's irritation, they weren't satisfied with keeping the information to themselves. Word got out and Suzy found herself the focus of the news media. As a result, she and Fin gained national notoriety as the people who could talk to ghosts and send them on their way. A few even borrowed the title of a TV series and started calling them the Ghost Whisperers.

After his experience, Fin's feelings about the ability became a bit more ambivalent. When he moved in with Suzy, he suggested that they make use of their fame and form a company. He suggested SpiritSent, a play on words focusing on the results they got, sending the ghosts away to the next plane of existence. Ghostbusters was already taken, he pointed out with some chagrin. Suzy was less than enthusiastic.

It didn't help that a lot of people began thinking of Suzy as a typical spirit medium and wanted her to put them in touch with dead loved ones. She got tired of explaining that that wasn't what she did. After a while, however, the calls tapered off as the continuous news cycle focused on other things.

Still, as the months passed, they had answered a couple of legitimate calls about hauntings and, together, had performed what Fin began calling send-offs. They hadn't charged anything for the service. Was there even a going rate for sending a ghost through the door into the next realm?

When asked about the cost for their service, Suzy felt content telling them to make a donation to BoatUS Foundation, a non-profit organization dedicated to promoting boating safety, in Mark and Emma's memory.

Aside from that, though, their lives took on a pleasant monotony. As they both tended to be homebodies, the sameness of their days suited them very well. Suzy worked sporadically at the local museum, while Fin worked on his latest book, and they would spend their afternoons and evenings together.

By the time summer rolled around, they were perfectly and happily situated in their routine.

2

D o you know what today is?" Fin asked. Suzy lazily turned her head and looked at him from under the wide-brimmed hat she wore, protecting her face from the bright, seaside sunlight. Her expression looked mildly curious, but under the scorching heat of the July sun, she seemed unable to verbally respond. "This is the three-year anniversary of when we first sat here looking out over the harbor together."

"Oh my god," Suzy exclaimed slothfully, "you remember the date?"

"I didn't," Fin smiled, "but Facebook reminded me. My Memories page showed me the photo I shared, which I took from this very spot."

"You and your Facebook," Suzy scoffed.

"Yeah, well your social life might profit by a little extra effort on your part," Fin countered.

"Nah," she shook her head, turning it back and resting it on her chaise lounge. "I'm too private."

A few moments of silence passed while they both relaxed, looking out over the harbor from the rooftop deck of Suzy's family home on Marblehead Neck, a few miles north of Boston.

"I did *kind of* remember, though," Fin said, "within a day or two."

"I thought so," Suzy snickered, turning toward him again. "You're so sentimental." Aware that she tended to be a smartass, she made sure to temper her comment with a smile.

"Is that what you love about me?" Fin asked.

Suzy's eyebrows pinched together as she looked at him.

"It's one of the things. Why?"

"I don't know," he shrugged. "I've just always been so plagued with self-doubt. I wonder what you see in me."

"Oh, Fin," Suzy sighed, taking a serious tone. She pushed herself up a little and consciously fought the somniferous effects of the sunlight. "There's just so much. You may not see it yourself, but it comes out in so many ways. You're intelligent, especially for someone who never went to college."

That was something that had always bothered Fin. His hyper-religious upbringing didn't allow for higher education. Since he had experienced bullying and other issues in school, at the time, he didn't really want to continue with more schooling, anyway. But his lack of a college education had gotten in the way of some job opportunities in the past. Still, he displayed a love of knowledge by being a voracious reader, and by his almost excessive research for his novels.

"You're kind and thoughtful," Suzy continued, "almost to a fault. If something comes down to being between your preference and someone else's, you usually allow the other person's preference. And that's especially the case if the other person is me.

"Some might say that's a weakness, but I don't see it that way. Because you've demonstrated moral strength when it matters, when it's not just a matter of preference. And you've exhibited strength in helping and protecting me, like when we went face to face with Liam's evil twin Duncan, and with Birdsong's nemesis Stone Face."

She smiled at him again.

"And like I said a minute ago, you're so sentimental."

"Yeah?" Fin replied. "Well," he took a deep breath, "if you think *that* was sentimental, I suggest you brace yourself, darlin'."

Suzy frowned and looked at him quizzically as he stood up. She was a little alarmed by the look of near-terror in his eyes. He turned toward her, and knelt down. Suzy's breathing quickened when he took her hand.

"Suzy Quinn," he said, his voice quivering, "I've admired you since I first met you, in that Dunkin' Donuts near the airport. Even before that, really, when we just knew each other online, when all I had was that silly picture you sent me with your eyes crossed and your tongue sticking out. Your strength, your empathy, your beauty, both inside and out, have made me see how perfect you are."

"I'm not perfect," she protested quickly but quietly, shaking her head.

"You're perfect for me," Fin replied immediately.

"Okay," Suzy conceded weakly. It was a discussion they had had numerous times.

"That admiration is still there," Fin continued undeterred, "but something else has grown alongside it, now. Suzy, I love you more than I've ever loved anyone or anything, even my 1962 first edition Spider-Man."

Suzy smiled, relaxing just a bit.

"You've gotten through some unbelievably hard times, and come through them amazingly well." Suzy wasn't so sure about that. She looked askance at him, but he continued before she could say anything. "And you've gotten me through some tough times, too. All of that has made me see that I always want you on my side." He held her hand a little tighter. "And *by* my side.

"Suzy, will you please marry me?"

Suzy exhaled and allowed her head to fall back on the chaise lounge, a tear dribbling down from each eye.

"I know you still love Mark," Fin quickly added, "and I don't intend to try to take his place. I'll always be a little jealous of him for finding you first, and for holding on to your love for all this time, in spite of everything, but—"

"Oh, Fin," Suzy fussed, "be quiet. You're right, I do love Mark, and I always will. That's not what my hesitation was about. I've come to know you very well in the last few years, which is how I could respond so thoroughly a few minutes ago when you asked what I saw in you. So, I've thought about this moment for a while, and what I would say. And I had it all figured out. I'm just a little dismayed that my snark has abandoned me."

Fin smiled nervously, unable to read in her face what her answer might be.

"As we've talked about before, I've known for a while that I love you, and that you were the one I wanted to be with. Hell, I remodeled and redecorated my whole house just to get Mark out of it and to open it up for you. And I know the kind of values that you were raised with. While I don't agree with the religious beliefs and the culture that accompanied those values, I do appreciate the person that you became because of them.

"You're my favorite smartassery target. One of the best things is that you don't get offended, but you actually seem to appreciate my dubious sense of humor, and you even serve some of it back to me. I can't imagine ever finding another person like you." She hesitated for a bit, then relented. "A more *perfect* person."

Fin looked at her for a moment.

"So, is that a yes?"

"Yes," Suzy smiled, "that's a yes."

The emotion that filled Fin's heart tumbled out in the form of laughter. He grabbed her, pulling her toward him in an enthusiastic embrace, punctuated by kisses and more laughter, some of it coming from Suzy.

Finally, Fin leaned back and looked at Suzy, his face still beaming. He got up off his knees, making an 'old noise,' and sat back down on his chaise lounge. He allowed his eyes to linger on her and he sighed.

Suzy looked expectantly at him, and Fin shook his head.

"I'm at a loss for words," he shrugged.

"But you're a writer."

"I know. If this was a scene I was writing, I would just end the chapter and start the next scene. It seems like this scene is ending with a bit of an anticlimax."

"Real life obviously needs better writers," Suzy replied.

Her phone rang to life on the table between them.

"A phone call works," Fin nodded.

Suzy grinned as she picked up her phone. She didn't recognize the number.

"Hello?"

"Is this Suzy Quinn?" asked a woman's voice.

"Yes, it is."

"Hi, Suzy." Her tone was tentative. "This is Joan Rossi. I'm Michelle Rossi's mother."

"Oh, hi," Suzy said with a little forced enthusiasm. She had never met Joan, and hadn't heard from Michelle in years. She frowned at Fin and shook her head as if it was the last person she would have expected to hear from, which was accurate.

"Suzy, Michelle told me that she hasn't been in contact with you in a long time, but she wanted me to call you." There was a long pause during which Joan took a deep breath and blew it out. "Michelle passed away a few days ago." Her voice cracked, and Suzy's manner instantly changed.

"Oh no, I'm so sorry."

"Thank you."

"She told you before she died that she wanted you to call me?" Suzy asked, her eyebrows creased.

"No," Joan said, and left another long pause. "She told me this morning."

Now it was Suzy's turn to pause.

"You've been in contact with her?"

"Actually, she's been in contact with me."

3

Suzy appreciated the fact that Fin enjoyed cooking their breakfast, and she allowed him to spoil her whenever the inclination struck him. She sat at the counter and watched him as he cooked the blueberry pancakes.

He didn't mix the blueberries in the batter. That made oddly-shaped pancakes with haphazardly-placed blueberries. Instead, he poured some batter into the pan, then manually placed blueberries into it, one by one, evenly spacing them around the pancake. This method appealed much more to his perfectionism. He picked up the spatula to be ready when the pancake needed to be turned.

He looked over at Suzy, ready to say something, but his train of thought was momentarily derailed when he saw the sexy and adoring look on her face. But with a little mental cajoling and finagling, he managed to get his thoughts back on track.

"I'm sorry I can't go with you," he said.

He had to leave in a couple of hours to fly to California. Daryl, his agent in Hollywood, had notified him that a production company called Intrepid Studios had a movie in preproduction, based on a screenplay that was suspiciously similar to one of Fin's earlier novels, *DragonCache*. Casting calls were going out, and Daryl thought that it would be expedient for Fin to be present as legal proceedings were initiated against the offending production company.

"That's okay," Suzy replied. "What you have to do is important." Fin nodded. "Are you nervous?"

"A little," Fin said. Suzy saw the spatula vibrate in his hand and knew he was more than just *a little* nervous. "But, it's not like I'm going to be fighting Intrepid on my own. Universal's lawyers will be there, too." He tried to take a deep cleansing breath, but it ended up being pretty shallow. Suzy decided she needed to get his mind off of it, at least for a bit.

"Any regrets about proposing?" Suzy asked.

"Only one," Fin replied with a frown. "I don't know if I was unsure of your answer, but I wish I'd gotten you a ring. In the movies, they always have a ring ready to go on the woman's finger." His voice sounded a little stronger, his grasp on the spatula a little steadier, and she smiled.

"Plenty of time for that. I meant are you nervous about getting married?"

Fin looked up at Suzy again.

"To you? Not a bit." His response was firm, immediate.

Suzy gazed at him for a few moments, taking in his stance in front of the stove. He always seemed so comfortable in the kitchen, and she enjoyed watching him. Seeing his earlier nervousness dissipate made her feel better.

"Would you be terribly disappointed if I didn't take your name?" she asked.

He looked at her for a few moments, thinking, then shook his head.

"No, I guess not. Why would you not, though?"

"Have you ever changed your name?"

"Have you forgotten who I am?" Fin asked.

Fin MacKinley had gained his fame and fortune writing under the pseudonym Michael Jones, a state of affairs that caused him a measure of consternation. As an artist and an introvert, the incongruity of both craving and fearing the spotlight created an internal conflict that he had yet to come to terms with. Having this Michael Jones character reaping his fame caused a weird mix of jealousy and relief.

"Sure, but you just had to create an alias at your bank. You didn't actually change your name. When women change their names because of marriage, or for whatever reason, it requires an exhausting mountain of paperwork –

with banks and credit cards and licenses and Social Security and an endless stream of other places that have their names on file. And it seldom goes smoothly. It's ridiculous."

"Yeah, I guess it would be," Fin agreed. "But no, I certainly wouldn't require that you take my name. I think I'm enough of a feminist to recognize that your rights and preferences are just as valid as mine." He flipped a pancake, then paused, turning to look at Suzy again, his eyes narrowed in a devious expression. "You know what? Maybe I should take *your* name."

"Why?" Suzy asked, looking at him as if he had sprouted a third foot from his forehead.

"Since I was involved in that tragic religious mishap, getting myself shunned, I'm basically dead to my family, so I have no familial connection to the name MacKinley. I'm in a new place, now, starting a new life. I don't even write under my own name. What good is it doing me?"

"Hmm," Suzy pondered as she looked at him. "Fin Quinn."

Fin frowned back at her.

"Okay, clearly, I haven't thought this through all the way."

Suzy smiled as he placed the last pancake on the plate that he had been keeping warm in the oven, and he turned off the burner under the skillet. He slid two of slices of bacon each onto two plates, then carried them into the dining room, placing them at their usual places. Suzy followed with the plate of pancakes.

The room, including the furnishings, the wall décor, even the finishes on the woodwork and the wide-planked floor looked almost exactly as it had in the early 1800s, when she saw it through the eyes of Fiona, her first ghost. The addition of plush cushions were the main difference, one which Suzy insisted on. She remembered the feeling of sitting on the hard chairs, though she remembered feeling it through Fiona's bottom, with Robert Drummond, the owner of the house at that time.

With sunlight streaming through the window, Fin and Suzy enjoyed their breakfast together before they had to separate.

4

J oan," Suzy said, "I don't understand. I barely knew Michelle." They were sitting in Joan's living room. Suzy had expressed her sympathy for Joan's loss, and they were now talking, a little awkwardly, over some tea. There was a subtle scent of sandalwood in the house, but Suzy didn't see incense burning anywhere.

Joan Rossi lived in Saugus, a northern suburb of Boston. Her house was a small Cape Cod in a neighborhood of modest Cape Cods and old-growth maple trees.

"Hmm," Joan replied, confusion showing in her red-rimmed, bloodshot eyes. "I don't know. I just know that Michelle *really* insisted that you be notified. I figured you must have been a good friend of hers."

Joan nervously ran her fingers through her greying brownish hair. She was attractive, and seemed nice, perhaps a little timorous and mousy. Suzy wondered if, maybe, "nutjob" could be added to the description. She had never heard of a ghost requesting that a relative contact a spirit medium. It was always the living, the survivors, who felt they needed that contact.

"I mainly knew her through mutual friends," Suzy said. "When my husband and daughter died a few years ago, I kind of withdrew from just about everybody. I'm ashamed to say that I lost contact with almost all my friends, and I haven't seen Michelle in even longer."

"Hmm," Joan replied again as she took a sip of tea.

"If you don't mind my asking, how did Michelle die?"

Joan sniffed and nodded, setting her cup down.

"Well, if you knew her at all, you knew she was a wild one." Suzy remembered. Joan pulled a tissue from the box next to her chair and dabbed at her eyes. "She moved out almost the very moment she turned eighteen. She never missed a chance to go to a party, and from what I've heard, she almost never went home alone. She drank like a fish, and I suspect she was into drugs, too.

"I didn't have any influence over her," she shrugged. "When I did see her, I'd try to talk some sense into her, but that just seemed to drive her further away from me. She stopped calling me, stopped coming by. She wouldn't answer my calls, and after a while, the only knowledge I had of her was what I heard from others.

"All through her twenties and thirties, Michelle kept up that lifestyle. I don't know how she did it, but she apparently managed to hold down a job. Someone called her a high-functioning alcoholic, and that seemed to fit.

"But she never slowed down," Joan sighed, "until she had to. She started having health issues, frequent bouts of weird and seemingly unrelated illnesses. That's when she discovered she was HIV-positive. She'd had so many sexual partners, there was no telling where it came from, but she probably infected tons of men since then. Or maybe it was from the drugs. I don't know."

Joan shook her head and looked down at her hands as they shook nervously in her lap. She wrapped one hand around the other and squeezed, temporarily calming the agitation.

"I only found out about it when she collapsed and an ambulance took her to the hospital. She was unconscious when she got there. The hospital tried calling a couple of numbers on her emergency contact list and didn't get an answer. I guess I was still on the list, farther down, so the hospital called me.

"Apparently, Michelle knew about the HIV for a while. Her doctor had started her on treatment, but my little girl just couldn't give up the drinking and the drugs. I don't know if that affected the success of the treatment, or if she just wasn't very careful about taking it. Knowing her, maybe both. But by the time the hospital called me, she was in full-blown AIDS.

"The poor thing was such a mess. I hardly recognized her. She'd lost so much weight, she almost looked like someone in those old pictures of Nazi concentration camp inmates.

"Well, I brought her back here to her own home so she'd be more comfortable, to care for her in what time she had left."

"Oh, so this is her house?" Suzy asked.

"Yes, it was. She was in no condition to fight me on it. I mean, she still did, but she didn't have the strength to win. She was my baby girl, and I was going to take care of her. Where else could she go? This was her house."

She took a deep breath and sighed heavily.

"She lasted about two weeks, and then she just died in her sleep."

Joan dabbed at her eyes again.

"I'm so sorry," Suzy said quietly, and she felt a prickling sensation down the back of her neck. She reached her hand up and gave her neck a rub, hoping to prevent a noticeable shiver. She frowned and wondered if the sensation had come from Michelle.

"Thank you," Joan replied. She leaned forward in her chair and looked at Suzy as she bunched her eyebrows together. "So, are you an exorcist or something like that?"

"No," Suzy shook her head, still rubbing the back of her neck a little nervously, "an exorcist is someone who is believed to be able to expel the devil or demons from a person they've taken possession of. What I do is make contact with the spirit of someone who's died and try to show them that they don't have to stick around here, that they can move on to the next realm."

Joan nodded, and Suzy looked at her emphatically.

"Now, you said that Michelle has been in contact with you. How, exactly has she made contact?"

Joan took a deep breath and blew it out, sitting back in her chair.

"I've heard her voice, usually accompanied by the smell of incense."

Suzy nodded. That explained the sandalwood she had smelled earlier.

"Sometimes it was just like random words and thoughts, some I couldn't even make out. But sometimes, it was like I just knew that she was talking to me. This morning was one of those times." Joan looked at Suzy pointedly. "In fact, she was screaming at me. Apparently, we still don't get along." She raised her eyebrows and sighed. "I'm afraid I haven't gotten much sleep since Michelle died. Anyway, this morning, she said, 'Call Suzy Quinn.' I said, 'Who?' She said, 'Suzy Quinn, the ghost whisperer.'"

Suzy shifted nervously in her seat.

"Okay, just to be clear, Joan, we aren't calling ourselves that. I'm sure that's a copyrighted name, and we could likely get in a lot of trouble if we used it for ourselves."

"I understand," Joan nodded. "But it made me know who she was talking about."

"Did she say why she wanted you to call me?"

"No, but since I'd seen a little about you on TV, I assumed she wanted your help getting out of here, moving on to the next realm, as you called it." She dabbed at her eyes again and sniffed. "I just want my little girl to finally find some happiness."

5

"hy does my baby girl need to go through all of that again?" Joan asked, distressed, as Suzy settled back into the wing-back chair. Suzy had just explained to her how the episodes work, that Suzy would see and experience whatever Michelle showed her, from Michelle's perspective, as if it was happening to Suzy. "She had such a hard life," Joan went on. "Can't you just tell her to go into the light, or something like that?"

"Well, it's not as simple as that," Suzy replied. "Spirits who remain in their physical vicinity, in the earthly realm, usually have unfinished business keeping them here. Regrets about how ties with a friend or relative were left, for instance. From what you told me about your relationship with her, I'm guessing maybe she'd like to rectify that before she moves on."

Joan pursed her lips in an expression of trepidation as she dabbed her eyes with a tissue.

"Does this really work?" she asked. "I've never believed in this afterlife stuff."

"I never did either," Suzy replied honestly. "But I was forced to change my mind a few years ago." Joan looked doubtful. "Don't worry, Joan," Suzy said soothingly, attempting to calm her concerns, "Michelle doesn't have to show me anything that's too difficult for her."

Joan nodded.

"What should I do?"

"Just do whatever you would do if I wasn't here. Once I'm in the episode, I won't hear you, so just go about your business."

Joan took a deep, shuddering breath and nodded. Her cheeks puffed out as she blew out the breath, and she looked around as if trying to decide what she should be doing, then she went into the kitchen.

Suzy sat back and sighed. She was relieved. Joan was a nice lady, but her daughter had only died a few days before, and the sadness was raw. Her emotions were strong and fresh, and Suzy could see a very real possibility of them interfering with her connection.

She closed her eyes and took a couple of deep breaths, feeling herself relaxing. She remembered when she started out, she needed a candle or some other flame to focus on. Now, she just opened her mind to the spirit world, and within a few seconds, she saw Michelle.

She, or rather, her apparition was the same pretty young woman Suzy remembered from a few years before. Except that something was different about her. It took Suzy a moment to recognize. It was the sadness that resided in Michelle's eyes.

Michelle had seemed like a carefree sprite, happy to be in whatever moment she was in. But Suzy knew the drinking, drugs and promiscuity suggested that the happiness was only a façade, showing only on the surface, a cover for a deeper disorder.

Michelle didn't say anything, just looked sadly at Suzy, and Suzy had the fleeting thought that Michelle's unfinished business might be with her. Just as she was about to ask about it, Suzy felt the swirling disorientation settling over her as she entered the episode.

§

Michelle studied her face in the mirror, putting the finishing touches on her makeup. She was satisfied with how she looked, for the most part. Her hair was styled nicely, every golden strand in place. Her face looked good. She was naturally pretty. The makeup she used was mainly to cover the dark circles that had taken up residence under her eyes.

Her eyes were the problem, the crimson roadmaps tracing their way around her blue irises. She reached for the eye drops she kept handy and squeezed a couple of drops into each eye. She couldn't worry about that now. Move on and finish getting ready while the eye drops got the red out.

She came out of the bathroom and into the bedroom as the smoke wafted sinuously around her. She had started burning incense years before, when she still lived at home. At that time, she used it to try to mask her marijuana use from her mother. In the process, she discovered that she loved the smell of sandalwood incense, and often burned it even when not partaking of the herb.

It helped to calm her, but not enough. She saw the bong on top of her dresser. Maybe just a quick hit to calm her nerves. She flicked the lighter, touching the flame to the weed in the bowl, and inhaled. She held it, then slowly exhaled, and she immediately felt better, more relaxed.

She sighed, then went into her closet. She pulled out the little black dress that she had planned on wearing and looked it over, then decided against it. It was sexy. Really *fucking sexy!* Maybe a little too much for a first date. For this first date, anyway. She wanted to get laid, but she wasn't sure this guy would respond positively to her piling it on so thick.

He seemed sweet. Most of the guys she had hooked up with through the dating site were out for one thing, and she had been fine with that. She wanted the same thing. Dinner, maybe a movie, if they lasted that long. A line or two of blow if they were up for it – and they usually were – then the clothes flew off and they were in bed rutting like dogs in heat.

It was rare that they spent the night. Usually, their clothes were back on within the hour and they were out the door, leaving Michelle alone. A kiss, maybe a promise to call. Sometimes they did, often they didn't. If they did, it was usually to hook up again for a repeat performance. And it was fairly rare that she didn't accommodate.

But an acquaintance had recently got her thinking seriously about her life. Was this really the way she wanted to grow old? The drinking, the drugs, the men. That lifestyle appealed to her now, or at least it was what she had become accustomed to. But she had noticed lately that it was starting to wear on her. A stable relationship with a nice man who wanted to grow old with her had begun to bear a certain appeal. Maybe it was time for her to settle down.

So, she started looking for a different kind of man, one who wanted a relationship rather than just a quick fuck. She spent some time thoughtfully altering her profile page, then saved it, watching to see what results it brought.

A few of them were horndogs hiding behind the relationship façade, and the sex had been pretty good. But it hadn't gotten her any closer to the stable lifestyle she wanted to try. Others were a little overeager, latching on to her within a day or two as if she were "the one" which, not surprisingly, turned her off big time.

Then, she saw this guy. He seemed truly nice, a gentleman, if such a thing still existed. They had talked on the phone a couple of times, and the gentleman exterior seemed to be genuine. He was interested in the whole "growing old together" thing.

She agreed to give it a try.

They met at a Starbucks and chatted over coffee for at least two hours. She was amazed when their first date was over and she wanted to see him again. In the moments when she was honest with herself, she was even more amazed that he wanted to see her again.

She decided on the light blue dress. It was sexy, too, but more subdued. If they ended up in bed together tonight, she wouldn't be disappointed. But if they didn't, well, she had to admit she wasn't sure. She hoped he liked her, and wanted her, too. She definitely wanted to fuck him. But if he wanted to wait a little, she'd just have to see how she felt about that when the time came.

She certainly didn't trust herself to say no.

Michelle pulled the dress on and looked at herself in the mirror. She looked damn good. She reached into the dress and pulled each of her breasts toward the center of her bra, increasing the effect of her cleavage, and nodded at the results.

She heard the doorbell and the anxiety came over her again. One more hit on the bong, then she tossed a mint in her mouth and careened down the stairs. She pulled the front door open, and there he was, smiling at her. God, he was so good looking!

31

"Hi, Michelle," he said. Then, his eyes traveled down her body and back up. "Damn!" Michelle smiled at his reaction.
"Hi, Mark."

§

Suzy grasped the arms of the chair, feeling as if she had been thrown bodily out of the episode and smashed against the wall. Her eyes were like saucers, her breathing shallow and nervous. She felt as if her body was heavy, weighed down by the grief and anxiety that suddenly flooded her system.

She looked around and didn't see Joan, but she heard the sounds of her puttering around in the kitchen. She was glad. She didn't want to have to explain what she had just seen.

She had forgotten that Mark had dated Michelle before Suzy met him. That in itself wasn't an issue. She knew that she herself and Mark had both had romantic entanglements before meeting each other. But seeing him in front of her now, alive and smiling, hearing his voice, speaking to her nearly five years after he had died was almost more than she could bear.

The fact that it was actually Michelle that he was looking at, smiling at, speaking to, meant little to Suzy at this point considering that it was Michelle's eyes that Suzy was seeing through. It was through Michelle's body that Suzy felt that tingle when Mark looked her up and down. And it was Michelle's lungs that had expanded in that reflexive sigh.

Suzy knew it wasn't real. What she had just experienced took place, she estimated, about fifteen years before. She was seeing someone else's flashback, a dead person's memory of another dead person.

But it was Mark.

Something that had tormented her so much after she developed her SpiritSense abilities, exactly a year after her husband and daughter died, was that she could see other dead people, experience their lives, but she could never see Mark or Emma again. It was so unfair.

Now, she felt as if she was being given the chance, even if it was a second-hand encounter. She had an opportunity to be with Mark again, to spend time with him, to talk to him.

In a way.

She knew she couldn't tell Joan, though. She didn't really know anything about any established rules of protocol or ethics for people in the paranormal field, but she figured that this would probably be bending a few.

She also knew she couldn't tell Fin.

Oh god, what about Fin? She had agreed to marry him, and now she was scheming to see her dead husband behind Fin's back.

Of course, she knew it wasn't that simple. The truth was actually more complicated and convoluted. And weird. She was temporarily inhabiting the memory of Michelle's body in order to spend time with Mark, as Michelle.

She sighed, then sat back, trying to relax enough to begin another episode.

6

I grew up in Boston," Mark was saying, "but I've lived in Charlestown for the last few years. Thing is I can do what I do from pretty much anywhere, as long as I have an internet connection."

Michelle looked across the table at Mark. He was a genuinely nice guy, but with an occasional good-natured smartass quality. Michelle was struggling to keep her craving in check. She really liked him. She didn't want to screw it up with him.

"I still don't understand," she said, "what exactly is it you do?" Mark smiled.

"It varies. I guess you could say I'm sort of a serial entrepreneur. The project I'm working on at the moment is called Peer. The name is a play on words, because it means both 'friends' and 'to watch.' It's a television streaming service that allows subscribers to connect with friends, recommend and share programs, things like that. Even watch shows together online. Kind of like Facebook TV.

"Before that, I wrote an accounting program that allowed users to personalize their options based not only on the needs of their field of work, but their specific business. I guess I get bored easily, so I like being able to sell what I've done and move on to my next idea."

"Well, damn," Michelle cooed, "look at the brain on you."

"Yeah, well it could just as easily be that I can't hold down a job." Mark cocked an eyebrow at her. "Your mother probably told you to watch out for guys like me."

"Hmm," Michelle replied, trying to fight off the expression of disgust, "reason enough to shitcan that warning."

"Uh-oh. Don't get along with your mom, huh?"

"Not exactly. My mother's a – Never mind. I don't want to talk about my mother. What about you? I suppose your family's as perfect as you are?"

"Perfect?" Mark scoffed. "You don't know me very well."

"Not yet." Michelle hoped that her remark didn't sound as libidinous as she felt. She picked up her glass, pausing as she saw the level of the Scotch. Their food hadn't even come yet and she was already almost through her double Scotch. Normally, that wouldn't be a problem, but with Mark, she was trying to make a better impression. She put the glass down and took a drink of her water.

She nervously looked up at Mark and, though he hadn't said anything, she noticed that her decision had not escaped his attention.

"Okay," she sighed, "time for full disclosure." She paused, looking down at her glass, hoping she wasn't about to screw it up with Mark. "I've been kind of wild. A couple of friends have made me see that, well, there's not much future in that kind of lifestyle. So, I'm working on cleaning up my act. Cutting down on the booze and the partying."

She looked back up at Mark, curious about his reaction. She was encouraged by the warm smile on his face.

"I think that's great," he said in a tone so warm, Michelle almost felt tears come to her eyes. "Like they say, admitting the problem is the first step to overcoming it."

Michelle didn't know how to respond, and she found herself just gazing into his kind eyes. Mark was the one to break the silence.

"If there's anything I can do to help, I'm happy to." He looked down, a little guiltily, at his own glass of Jameson. "Maybe drinking in front of you isn't the best course of action."

"Oh no," Michelle said quickly, reaching over to touch his hand, "please don't feel bad about that. I mean it's not like I'm on the wagon." She nodded down at her own glass. "Obviously. I'm just trying to get it a little more under control."

"Well, good for you." Mark smiled at her. "And I meant what I said. I'm happy to help, to be an encouragement or whatever, if I can."

"Thank you, Mark," Michelle said, feeling herself get a little choked up. "I really appreciate that. That's so kind of you."

Mark shrugged somewhat self-consciously, as the waitress arrived with their food.

§

Michelle was anxiously waiting to see how the evening turned out. She felt almost ashamed to realize that she had stolen several glances at Mark's crotch when he wasn't looking. But he wasn't showing off, wasn't advertising what he was packing like so many of the guys she had been with. Her glances had revealed nothing, neither about his physical characteristics, nor his intentions for later.

Mark had taken her to dinner at a nice restaurant, followed by a moonlight walk along Revere Beach. Michelle wanted to remember everything about the evening.

She noticed the remaining glow of sunset dissipating over the buildings and the skeletal trees of Revere. There was a tangible texture to the night – more than just the physical qualities. A bit of humidity hung in the air, and she felt the chill, but there was more. She had heard people speak of electricity in the air, and she felt that now. Being near Mark, walking beside him, talking to him, she felt as if a current pulsed through her body. She had never experienced that with any other man before.

Then, he tentatively took her hand. He seemed truly interested in her as they talked about themselves, and she told him things that she had never told other men. In fact, few other men would have even cared to hear them. They completed their walk along the sea hand-in-hand. It was just like one of those sappy romantic ads. Everybody seems to love long walks on the beach.

As they were walking back toward the car, Michelle saw a homeless man on a corner. Immediately, she fished around in her purse and found a few singles, and she handed them to him. He thanked her, and she resumed her walk with Mark.

She noticed the cynical look on his face.

"What?" she asked.

"You know he's probably just going to go buy booze or drugs with that, don't you?"

"No, I don't know that," she replied, then immediately felt bad about the indignation that came out in her voice. She thought for a few moments. "I just think about what a mess I've been. Like the saying goes, 'But for the grace of God, that could be me.' Or something like that." She looked up at Mark. "Homeless people aren't just drug addicts waiting for their next fix. They're hungry, too. I gave that man an opportunity to make a choice. Everybody's fucked up in some way, some worse than others, obviously. But I think most people are basically good and deserve our help if we can give it."

"Wow," Mark said, and Michelle saw the admiration in his expression. "You're a modern-day Anne Frank."

"What do you mean?"

"While she and her family were in hiding from the Nazis in the Netherlands, and in fear for their lives, she wrote, 'I still believe, in spite of everything, that people are truly good at heart.' That was only a year or two before she died in the Bergen-Belsen concentration camp.

"I hate to admit it, but I'm cynical and sometimes tend to judge people based on first impressions. But you're like Anne Frank all grown up."

Michelle looked up at Mark, and his face blurred as her eyes misted a little.

"I'm almost afraid for you to get to know me," she replied quietly.

It really had been a lovely evening. She just didn't know how it was going to end up.

In her past life, she would have had no doubt. In fact, the walk along the beach probably wouldn't even have been a part of the evening. Discussions of personal philosophies or Anne Frank certainly would not have been.

They would have gone back to her place or his, likely depending on which was closer, perhaps another drink to loosen up a bit more. There would be some kissing, some caressing to further the mood, then their clothes would fall off and they'd be fucking. There was really no other word for it. It was seldom that "making love" came into play. It was simply pure animal sex, a satisfying of primal needs.

She had a feeling it wouldn't be that way with Mark.

As he pulled up in front of her house, he shut off the engine, glanced at her, then got out of the car. He walked around to her side, opening her door, and she felt like a princess or a dignitary of some kind. She didn't even realize men still did this.

He walked her to her door and, after she unlocked it, she turned to him. He took her hand again, then leaned forward. She leaned, as well, closing the distance, and their lips met. Though her guts were churning, wanting to feel his hands on her, to feel his body against hers, she waited, letting him take the lead.

It was a very chaste kiss, warm and soft, and terribly romantic, leaving her wanting more. Then, he pulled away, looked her in the eye, and he smiled at her.

"I'd like to see you again," he said.

"I'd like that, too," she said a little breathlessly.

§

Suzy's eyes were swimming in tears when she came out of the episode. Getting a glimpse of Mark at the end of the first episode had been a shock. But spending time with him now, talking to him, holding his hand, kissing him, was almost more than Suzy could bear. She knew it wasn't herself, but through Michelle's memory, and that in itself caused a strange dichotomy of emotions. She could feel Michelle's reactions to Mark, and she also felt her own, superimposed over them.

But still, it was Mark!

She sat back in the wing-back chair, trying to control her breathing, and she looked around. Joan still wasn't around, and Suzy could, again, hear her puttering in the kitchen. The woman loved baking, apparently, or whatever she was doing.

Suzy pushed herself up onto her feet, pausing as she felt her head spinning more than she had in a long time. When the room steadied again, she made her way through the dining room, toward where she heard Joan working in the kitchen. Joan looked up, surprised to see her.

"Oh," she said, "are you finished?"

"No," Suzy said, shaking her head, "I've only had a couple of episodes. But it's pretty draining on me, physically and emotionally, so I need to leave for a bit, to clear my head."

"Oh," Joan replied a little disappointed. "I was going to make brownies. But I guess you can have some when you get back." Joan puckered her eyebrows together. "You'll be back today, right?"

"Yes," Suzy said. "I just need to separate myself from the situation for a few minutes. And honestly, Joan, you don't need to be here. I mean it's entirely up to you, but I can make this connection whether you're here or not. So, if you need to get out of the house, run errands or do anything else, it's fine. As long as you're cool with me being here."

"Honey, I got no place to be." Joan smiled, pinkening her cheeks. "But thank you for being concerned about me."

Already tense from Joan's presence, Suzy was a little disgruntled by her response, but she smiled at her as she left.

7

It was a decent script. Fin hated to admit it, especially considering the glaring similarities to *DragonCache*. But Daryl, Fin's Hollywood agent, had gotten his hands on a copy of the script and overnighted it to him. And it was good.

Fin closed the folder and put his head back, remembering his thoughts about that earlier novel of his after *TimePlex* had been turned into a movie and become a huge success. He had wished that Peter Jackson, of *Lord of the Rings* fame, would discover *DragonCache*, the novel Fin thought was his best, and make a movie based on it.

He looked out the window of the plane and, judging by the terrain six and a half miles below him, figured he was probably flying over Kansas or Nebraska. He pulled his phone out, set to "Airplane Mode," and looked at the time. Still nearly three hours till he was scheduled to land at LAX.

He wondered how Suzy was doing. He wished he had been able to be there with her, to help her with the send-off. Especially since it was a friend. That would likely make it a particularly difficult case.

But he was always amazed at Suzy's strength and resilience. The things she had endured would have broken a lot of people. But Suzy came through it, certainly not unscathed, but unbroken, and with her snarky sense of humor intact. Even more amazing to Fin was that she was eventually able to love again. And that she had chosen him to be the one.

That, he thought, was the part that was bothering him the most about this trip, more than the copyright infringement case, even more than not being there with Suzy for

Michelle's send-off. But the fact that he had proposed, and Suzy accepted, and he immediately had to fly away on some mundane business matter. He wanted, more than anything, to be with Suzy, to celebrate their engagement.

He turned toward the window again, not really looking at anything. He sighed and picked up his glass, taking a sip of The Macallan 12-year-old Scotch. They didn't have his favorite, Ben Nevis 21-year-old, but he had to admit this was good. As the liquor burned a path down his throat, he decided to stop feeling sorry for himself.

He bent over and reached into his computer bag and pulled out a highlighter. He opened the script and began reading it again, marking bold yellow lines over the text that he knew was obviously copied from his book.

8

Suzy pulled her red and white Mini Cooper into one of the empty parking spaces lining the northbound lane of Revere Beach Boulevard. She got out of her car and looked at the William G. Reinstein Bandstand. Named for a former mayor of Revere, she recognized the gazebo in the episode she had just experienced. Michelle and Mark had walked along this very beach after dinner at the restaurant.

Suzy wandered past the structure and down onto the beach, watching the waves roll up onto the sand fifty yards out.

What the hell are you doing, Suzy? She sighed as she walked down toward the wet sand, currently out of reach of the waves, but where the footing was a little more solid. In her memory of the episode, she remembered Mark walking with her, holding her hand.

She knew it had actually taken place with somebody else fifteen years ago. But as far as Suzy was concerned, her physical sensations, her emotions, it was her own hand that Mark had held, just a few minutes ago.

Against her better judgment, she stopped and closed her eyes, reviewing the two episodes she had just experienced, particularly the second one, in which she had spent so much time with Mark.

In her mind, now, Michelle was barely there. Suzy herself is the one who had spent that time with him. She could still feel his hand, the shape and structure of it so clear in her memory, the softness of his caress still warming her skin.

She opened her eyes and looked around her. The difference was jarring. Even though nothing was said about the time of year, she had Michelle's knowledge that her first date with Mark had taken place in early April. The night had been a little chilly, and when Michelle shivered, Mark had noticed and suggested that they turn back. Michelle had hesitated, knowing that it might be the end of the date, but Suzy smiled warmly at the memory of Mark's thoughtfulness.

Now, as Suzy looked around, it was almost noon in July, and the beach was crowded with people. The sun was almost directly overhead, and she felt a drop of perspiration slither down her back. She took a deep breath and blew it out.

She needed to be more professional. Michelle had requested her help. That sort of thing never happened. Suzy needed to focus on Michelle's story and try to leave herself out of it.

She heaved a heavy sigh and turned around, walking back toward her car.

§

"God, you're incredible!" Michelle said as Mark lay there in her bed. She had started burning a stick of sandalwood incense on the headboard before they started. It was nothing but little bits of grey ash now, but the scent still lingered in the air of her bedroom. Sunlight streamed across them almost horizontally, translucent in the abiding incense smoke, as the sun peeked over the horizon. Mark's arm was under Michelle's neck, his hand caressing her upper arm, as she panted, trying to catch her breath.

Michelle's sexual experiences had seldom included a man being attentive to her needs and desires, and Mark had established himself as a trailblazer in that area, in her mind, at least. He had climaxed before her, but after that, he spent time making sure she came as well.

Other men she had taken to bed had been focused on satisfying their own desires, and if they spent any time bringing her to

43

climax, it had usually been at her own urging. With Mark, she didn't need to say a word. It was as if it was only natural. The sex wasn't just for him, but for Michelle, too. It was a package deal.

Mark turned toward her, looking at her from two inches away. Though Michelle said nothing about it, she noticed that he shaped his mouth in such a way as to direct his breath downward, so he wasn't blowing in her face. As was becoming a common occurrence, she was impressed by his thoughtfulness.

He smiled at her and, in lieu of a verbal response, he closed those two inches toward her and kissed her.

As the afterglow gradually faded, Michelle asked what Mark had planned for the day.

"Well," he sighed, "I need to start getting ready to move."

"Move?" Michelle said, pulling her head back a bit to be able to focus on his face better. Her eyebrows were scrunched together in a frown. "Where are you moving?"

"Oh, you know me. I'm a vagabond. Can't stay in one place for very long."

"Mark," Michelle said, lifting herself up on her elbow, her tone becoming more concerned, "no, I didn't know that about you at all."

"Okay, Michelle," Mark said in a calming voice, smiling, "we've been seeing each other for a few months. You should know by now that I'm a smartass." Michelle's face expressed a cautious change. "I've just started looking for a new place. My lease is up soon, and I'm not ready to buy anything yet."

"Okay," Michelle said, a relieved tone in her voice, as she relaxed, allowing her head to rest again on his shoulder. "But you're staying around here?"

"Yes, I'm staying around here." Mark smiled more broadly, perhaps, she thought, a little flattered that the idea of him moving away would cause such a reaction in her. Satisfied, Michelle snuggled back up to him, reveling in the feel of the closeness of their naked bodies.

Suddenly, she jerked away, peering excitedly into his eyes.

"Move in with me," she said.

44

"What?" Mark asked, turning his head to look at her. "You're crazy, woman. After only four months?"

"I'm serious. There's plenty of room here. I mean yes, it's a little house, but there's a small bedroom that I just use for storing shit I don't use. I can clear it out and you can use that as your office.

"Seriously, Mark, you've been so good for me. I told you when we first met that I wanted to come clean. Since you've been with me, I've been doing that. It's like just being with you has satisfied all my needs."

She felt a little guilty about that statement. It wasn't entirely true, though she had been doing much better. So, she decisively pushed that feeling out of the way.

"I don't know about that," Mark said skeptically. "But I'm glad that you've been able to clean up your life. Although your incense habit is a little concerning."

"Seriously, Mark, I couldn't have done it without you." She leaned up on her elbow and continued excitedly. "When I'm not with you, I feel those old cravings. I want to start using again. But when you're with me, I feel so calm and peaceful. It's like I don't need that shit at all." She placed her hand on his chest and tilted her head imploringly. "Really, Mark, I would love for you to move in here. We'll be so good for each other."

Mark smiled at her, and she felt her heart melting as his smile had done to her so many times before. Seeing his attitude soften a little, she continued.

"You need a place to live. And you told me yourself you can do your work from anywhere. I'll be at work during the day, and you'll have the place to yourself. Then we can be together in the evenings."

"Well, my work sometimes requires evenings, too," Mark replied.

"That's okay. I'll stay out of your way. But just having you around will be good for me."

He regarded her for a few moments, then he sighed.

"Let me think about it, okay?" Michelle smiled. A maybe was certainly a lot better than no.

"Okay," she said, settling back down against him. God, he ignited such a fire in her! Maybe if he was provided a little more incentive. She started rubbing her body against his, and she slipped her hand down his belly. She found what she was looking for. She started fondling him, and she smiled as she felt the stiffness gradually returning.

§

Suzy came out of the episode, and the house smelled wonderful, although she was a little surprised that it didn't smell of sandalwood. But she was chagrined to see Joan sitting across from her on the sofa, reading a magazine. She looked up when she sensed Suzy's return. Suzy squeezed her legs together, struggling to stifle the desire that was smoldering inside her, to quell that electrical current that coursed through her.

"There you are," Joan said, putting her magazine down. "There's a brownie and a glass of milk for you," and she motioned toward the coffee table in front of Suzy. Visiting with Joan was the last thing she wanted at a time like this, and she wasn't sure she could handle eating anything now, but she thought it might distract her mind a bit from the emotional flagellation she was enduring.

"Thank you," she smiled.

"So," Joan said as Suzy took a bite of brownie, "have you learned anything useful yet?"

Suzy knew she couldn't tell Joan, in detail, about what she had seen in the episodes so far, and she used the excuse of having her mouth full to stall, to think of something to say.

"Nothing yet," Suzy said after she swallowed, "but I'm beginning to believe that Michelle's 'unfinished business' is with me."

"Really?" Joan replied, her face expressing confusion. "I thought you said you didn't know her that well."

"That's true," Suzy agreed, "but I'm finding that we had a little more in common than I realized." She could see the

46

curiosity showing on Joan's face, and she continued before Joan could ask for an explanation. "I really can't comment on it yet. I need to let it play out, and then I'll have a better idea of how to send her on to the next plane."

"I see," Joan said, obviously disappointed, but she didn't press any further. "Well, whatever you can do to bring her some peace, I'd sure appreciate it."

Suzy smiled and nodded as she felt the tension settling in her shoulders.

9

I really wanted to hate it," Fin said. He was lying on the bed in his hotel room, his cell phone pressed against his ear, and though he wasn't aware of it, he was smiling as he talked to Suzy. "But it's a damn good script."

"It's your book?" Suzy asked.

"Well, the character names are different, and there are some story differences, as there always are with theatrical adaptations, but it's so apparent that they read *Dragon-Cache*. It's definitely my story."

"So, what do you think is going to happen?"

"I can't really say. I only talked to Daryl briefly when I got to my hotel, and he had something else going on and had to take another call. But he's still confident that we'll be able to crush Intrepid for their theft of my story. We're meeting with them tomorrow morning."

"That's great. Sounds like you might get a nice settlement out of it."

"Oh, I don't know about that."

"Really?" Suzy inquired. "You and Daryl sounded so sure."

"No, it's not that I'm not sure." Fin paused and thought for a moment. "The similarities are so obvious I don't think there's any way that a judge would believe that it's not my story.

"It's just that, I don't know, it seems like a David and Goliath story. They don't have a chance. Intrepid Studios is a small, independent company. From what I've heard, they have very little in the way of funding for the movie, let alone company capital. I'm thinking a 'cease and desist' might be the best that we can hope for."

"Aw, I'm sorry."

"Well, that's not even what has me down. I mean, seriously, I wasn't expecting to make a bundle from this showdown. I just didn't want someone else making unauthorized use of my work. But they're a small operation, and they did a great job on the screenplay. Having been an indie author for several years, you know I always tend to root for the underdog, especially when their work is good."

"But it's *your* work," Suzy pointed out.

"The *novel* is my work," Fin corrected. "I don't know the first thing about writing a screenplay. I'm too close to the story. I don't think *anything* should be cut. But, of course, it has to be to fit it into a two-hour movie. And they did it very well."

"Hmm," Suzy said. "Well, maybe this whole debacle will finally get Hollywood's attention focused on *Dragon-Cache*."

"Yeah, maybe," Fin agreed. Then, his voice brightened. "Hey, how was *your* day? How did the send-off go?"

"Well," Suzy began, choosing her words carefully, "it hasn't happened yet. It may take a little time. Michelle was such a mess."

"I'm so sorry I couldn't be there with you," Fin said. "I'm sure, being a friend, this one is more difficult than cases you've had in the past."

"She wasn't really a close friend," Suzy said, trying not to sound relieved that he wasn't there. "More like an acquaintance. But still, it's difficult seeing such a hard life play out in front of me."

She winced, feeling dishonest at her manipulation of the facts. It wasn't Michelle's hard life that was difficult, but Suzy's interaction with Mark.

She knew that Fin had a certain amount of built-in insecurity, partly related to his religious upbringing, and partly from past interactions with other women. But even without that, Suzy felt that her emotional indiscretions with the memories of a ghost were dancing around the fringes of ethics.

In fact, she hadn't even seen that much, yet, that pointed to a hard life. She had seen Michelle interacting with Mark.

Or rather, she saw herself interacting with him. She vigorously shook her head to try to remove the thoughts from her mind.

Before Fin could ask any more probing and potentially embarrassing questions, Suzy decided to change the subject. Ursula had climbed up in her lap, and Suzy snapped a picture of her and sent it to Fin. From that point on, the conversation was much lighter.

It didn't soothe Suzy's conscience at all, but at least she didn't dig herself any deeper.

10

I completely understand if you don't want to leave a virtual stranger alone in your house," Suzy said. Joan had just explained that she had to go back to work today.

Joan looked haggard as she pondered for a moment, standing in the open doorway of the house on Monday morning, glancing nervously behind her. Her eyes were dry, but still red, perhaps even more than the day before.

"I assure you my only goal here is to help Michelle to move on to the next plane," Suzy continued. "But it's entirely up to you."

"It's not that I don't trust you," Joan sighed. "I've just always been leery of allowing, as you said, 'strangers alone in my house.' But you were a friend of Michelle's so," she stepped aside and opened the door a little wider, "please come in."

"Thank you, Joan," Suzy said, smiling as she walked in.

"I'm sure it doesn't help that I haven't gotten much sleep," Joan said. "Michelle was, well, pretty belligerent during the night."

"Really?" Suzy replied, her eyebrows knitting together in puzzlement. The house felt calm now. She didn't know what Joan was referring to.

"I love my baby girl," Joan added, shaking her head, "but she could sure get herself in a state." She looked apprehensively around her. "When she did, she wasn't the easiest person to get along with."

Suzy looked around the quiet house, trying to see what Joan was looking for. But she realized that daughters often had issues with their mothers that others might know nothing about. Her main concern was the unfinished business that Michelle had with her.

"I sure hope you can help Michelle find some peace and move on soon," Joan implored.

"I honestly don't know how long it will take, but I'm sure it will depend on how quickly I can resolve whatever issues that Michelle has with me. I'm afraid it's not an exact science. I'm picking it up as I go."

Joan asked if Suzy needed anything before she left. Suzy declined as she settled back into the wing-back chair she had occupied yesterday. Joan nodded, looked around again, then she said goodbye and left.

Suzy took several deep breaths as she looked at her surroundings. She realized that her shoulders were 'up around her ears,' as her mom used to say. She forced herself to relax them, then, to her surprise, she smelled a subtle scent of sandalwood. She sighed and closed her eyes, relaxing her whole body, as she felt the episode wrapping itself around her.

§

Michelle handed a five dollar bill to the man sitting on the corner near where she had parked. The salon was near a busy intersection, and there was usually a homeless person stationed on at least one of the corners.

She crossed the street to where she had parked, and she got into her car, reached into the glove compartment, and pulled out a clear plastic tube. Pulling off the top, she tipped it over into her hand, and she lit up the joint, taking a long drag on it, holding it in her lungs. As the stress of the day was supplanted by a feeling of calm, she felt ready to make the drive home.

She felt a twinge of guilt as she experienced the effects of the marijuana permeating her body. She knew that some people considered pot to be just as bad as coke or speed, but Michelle just used it occasionally to relax after a difficult day. Still, it was an illegal substance, although there was talk recently about legalizing it.

But she hadn't specifically included it in her talks with Mark about "cleaning up her life." She didn't know for certain how he would consider that loophole of omission, though he did, she remembered, seem to disapprove of the bong in her bedroom, enough that she had moved it out of there.

Michelle hadn't been able to afford a university education. But she had put herself through a cosmetology course at the community college. It wasn't the schooling she had hoped for, but it was the best that she could do. Having received her certificate a few years before, she had been able to finally position herself in a nice beauty salon in Charlestown.

Despite her self-destructive proclivities, she enjoyed her work and applied herself to doing a good job, even if she did have to take a little snort once in a while to get herself through the day. She was gregarious and her clients liked her, so she had more than enough work to support herself. Still, it always felt good when she could take off.

In the past, she would often go straight to a party, or meet up with friends at a local bar. This evening, though, she was heading home. Mark had just moved in, and she was looking forward to going home to him. This was the first day she had left him alone at her house, and she felt particularly domestic and respectable going home to him for the evening.

She carefully tamped out the last half of the joint in the ashtray and dropped it back into the tube, sighing at the resurgence of the guilt. She popped a breath mint, started her car and pulled out onto Rutherford to begin her drive north toward home.

§

Something seemed off when Michelle pulled up in front of her house. She couldn't quite tell what it was. She looked around the neighborhood. A couple of houses still had Halloween decorations up, glowing orange in the darkness. She had never bothered with that, and her house looked pretty much the way it always did.

For the most part.

She noticed a lot of lights were on, though, nearly every window lit up. As she approached the front stoop, she saw the broken pot, the dirt and the dead zinnias that never really took root scattered across the walk.

53

She opened the door and went inside. As she pushed the door closed behind her, Mark suddenly came around the corner, looking anxiously toward the door. There was a bruise forming around his right eye and a trickle of blood from his nose.

"Oh my god!" Michelle squealed, rushing toward him. "What happened?"

"You had a caller," Mark replied with a bitter, accusing tone, his voice sounding a little nasal, as if he had a cold. He dabbed at the blood running down from his nose. "Who's Nicky?"

"Shit," Michelle said under her breath. She turned Mark by the shoulder and marched him toward the bathroom. "What did he want?"

"Said he needed some blow. Said you always got it for him." Michelle got a tissue and began dabbing at the blood below his nostril. "Are you a dealer, too?" Michelle stopped and looked him in his rapidly discoloring eye, an expression of shame showing on her face.

"Nicky's my brother." She dribbled a little water from the faucet onto the tissue to wipe the drying blood off of his lip. Her voice cracked a little as she continued. "He's even more fucked up than me. Can't hold onto a job, usually doesn't have enough to eat. I suspect he's living on the street."

"Oh," Mark breathed. Michelle watched for a couple of seconds and didn't see any new blood appear.

"What did you tell him?" she asked as she steered Mark toward the kitchen.

"I said you're not doing that anymore," Mark replied a little sheepishly, "and told him to stop coming around." Michelle looked at Mark as she got a dish towel, then she wrapped some ice in it.

She looked up at Mark and gently placed the ice against his eye.

"From the looks of your face, I take it he didn't just turn around and leave."

"No, he didn't. I'm afraid he seemed pretty desperate. He came at me with his arms flailing." Mark winced a little. "I landed a couple of pretty good punches myself before he left. He

54

tripped over a pot out on the front stoop and took off running down the street."

Michelle sighed.

"I'm sorry," Mark said. "I didn't know – well, I didn't know you even had a brother. You've never mentioned him."

"No," Michelle said, insistently shaking her head, "it's okay. You didn't do anything wrong. I'm just sorry he did this to you. I told him the last time I saw him that I was cleaning up my life, and I tried to convince him to do the same. I guess he didn't believe me."

"I've never been involved in that kind of life," Mark said as he eased himself down into a chair, "but I can't imagine it's an easy life to give up."

"No," Michelle agreed as she turned to the refrigerator, looking for something to start preparing for dinner.

"What about you, though?" Mark asked. "It doesn't seem to be that tough for you."

"Oh, I have my moments," she countered. She turned and looked at Mark, and she smiled. "It helps to have someone in my corner, rooting for me."

She turned back to the fridge, feeling a twinge of guilt about the small bump of coke she had dipped on her fingernail this afternoon to help her get through the rest of the day.

11

Fin settled back in the plush chair as he looked across the big impressive mahogany conference table in the legal department of Universal Studios. The representatives of Intrepid Studios were sitting across from him.

There were three of them. The one in the middle was John Whitson, the owner of the company and director of *Call of the Dragon*, the project that Fin was now convinced was based on his novel.

To Witson's right was Marion Plum, the screenwriter. She was a woman in her fifties with a pleasant face, and dark hair that was leaning toward the color of her name.

On Whitson's left was Jeremy Dyson, a lawyer who looked like he might be twenty-five, though figuring necessary time for a law degree and passing the bar, he was probably a little older. Fin didn't know if Dyson was regularly employed by Intrepid, or if they had just retained him for this case.

They all seemed somewhat intimidated.

On Fin's side was Daryl Higgins, his Hollywood agent, several executives from Universal Studios, and three lawyers, all dressed in expensive-looking suits. Fin wore his usual go-to 'business outside the house' attire, blue jeans, a casual shirt and a lightweight blazer, and thought he might be a little underdressed.

The table was decidedly lopsided, and Fin felt a little intimidated himself. But he was glad he was sitting on this side of the table.

"I'd like to thank you for agreein' to meet with us," started Randall Black, one of Universal's lawyers, and the one who seemed to be taking charge of the proceedings. He was fiftyish, with a southern accent, a deep, reverberating voice, and an encyclopedic knowledge of movies. His manner reminded Fin a little of Tommy Lee Jones, and he was glad he didn't have to face off against him. "Charges of plagiarism and copyright infringement are very serious. We were gonna slap a 'cease and desist' on you, with the usual, accompanyin' fines. But Mr. Jones over here displayed a commendable amount of fellow feelin'," he glanced at Fin, "so we agreed to do this little face-to-face. Besides, whenever possible, we want to avoid lengthy, expensive and potentially damaging lawsuits."

The three on the other side of the table glanced nervously at each other. Dyson cleared his throat and spoke up.

"Thank you," he started, his eyes darting back and forth at the people across from him. "First of all, I'm curious about why Universal is taking an interest in this? Are you producing a movie based on *DragonCache*?"

"Universal has no such production in the works as of yet," Black replied, "but we did produce the last two adaptations of Mr. Jones' novels. I guess you could say we're intervening here as a favor to Mr. Jones."

"I see," Dyson said. He looked across the table, steeling himself for the confrontation. "Well, I'd like to start out, if you don't mind, by pointing out that plagiarism is not a legal offense, but an academic one." He glanced nervously at his companions. "And perhaps an ethical one." Randall Black tilted his head curiously as he listened. "Plagiarism is something you hear about in colleges and universities, and the punishment for it can certainly be serious for the offender, including expulsion or revocation of a degree. But it's not a legal issue."

"Thank you for that, Mr. Dyson," Black replied easily and sincerely. Fin couldn't tell if the sincere tone was real or sarcastic. "But if you don't mind, I'd like to point out that your statement is inherently incorrect. There have been numerous legal precedents established in which plagiarism has indeed been proven to be a legal issue.

"While it's true that the act of plagiarizin' someone else's work is not, in and of itself, illegal, it can result in a heap o' trouble for the plagiarist, especially if it infringes on the original author's copyright.

"The owner of the copyrighted material, in this case, Mr. Michael Jones," Black gestured toward Fin, "could sue the pants off the plagiarist in federal court for violation of the copyright which he himself owns." He smiled at Marion Plum. "I assure you, Ms. Plum, I meant nothin' off-color by that remark."

Dyson shifted nervously, and Marion Plum looked at Fin. Fin saw fear in her eyes.

"Well," Dyson said, "we haven't established that there has even been copyright infringement."

"You're right," Black said quickly, jabbing his finger toward him in a bold gesture. "So, why don't we dig in and get started on that." He leaned forward to look around Daryl. "Mr. Jones, could we see that script you were nice enough to highlight for us?"

Fin quickly passed the screenplay to him, not wanting to keep him waiting. Black opened the screenplay and whistled in sarcastic amazement as he flipped through the pages, many of which were almost entirely yellow from Fin's highlighter. "It appears that Mr. Jones has found a few similarities."

Looking across the table, Fin almost felt bad for the 'little guys' facing the juggernaut of Randall Black.

12

Michelle woke up feeling particularly horny. She felt another need, too, but she tried to push that one aside. She really was trying to clean up her life, and she knew the drugs, when she let herself think about it, were not good for her.

Giving in to the other craving, though, she turned over and saw that Mark's side of the bed was empty. Frowning, she looked at the clock. It was 7:00 a.m. on a Sunday morning. She pushed herself up and got out of bed. She felt unsteady on her feet. She really needed a hit, but she resisted.

She went downstairs into the living room where she heard rustling sounds. Mark was there pulling on a jacket. When he looked up and saw her standing there wearing only a T-shirt, the carnal expression that came over his face only added fuel to her desire, but she was still stuck on the fact that he was leaving.

"Where are you going?" she asked.

"Hey babe," Mark replied. "Sorry, I left a note." He nodded toward a slip of paper on the coffee table. "I didn't want to wake you. I need to drive down to Providence. I may have a buyer for Peer." He smiled excitedly.

"On a Sunday morning?" she whined. "This is our time."

"I know," Mark said in a conciliatory tone. "I'm sorry. This came up unexpectedly. But I'll be back this afternoon. Maybe we can go out to dinner or something. Especially if I have something to celebrate." He smiled again and waggled his eyebrows.

Michelle tried to hold it together. Having pushed aside her body's earlier desire for a sniff, she had prepared herself to seduce Mark back to bed. Now, she wasn't getting that, either.

She had heard about the hypothesis of addictive personalities, and how some believe that a person may be predisposed to addictions of multiple kinds. In her own case, she could certainly believe it. Having had issues for years now with drugs and alcohol, and sex, she was now feeling her addiction to Mark growing.

She wondered if there was anything to it, and if so, if a benefi-cial addiction could be used to take the place of another more harmful one. If that was the case, maybe Mark really could help her get over her other addictions.

But now, her fix was leaving.

"Mark, I wanted to spend time with you today."

"I know, honey," Mark replied, coming to her and taking her into his arms. "I really am sorry. But I let you know from the start that I don't work regular hours." He kissed the top of her head. "We'll have this evening. And you don't work tomorrow, so we can spend the whole day together. Especially if this meet-ing goes the way I hope it does."

He lifted her face up toward his and kissed her. Then, he turned and walked out the door.

§

The depression that descended onto Michelle after Mark left only got worse. Enwrapped with a feeling of desperation, she col-lapsed into a chair, tears in her eyes, and masturbated furiously for a half hour until her hand was tired and her clit was sore, but she just couldn't bring herself to climax.

She wandered aimlessly around the house, still wearing only the T-shirt, not feeling motivated to get dressed. Mark had made a pot of coffee, and she drank what was left of that. It helped, but it wasn't enough.

She started another pot, and devoured a container of leftover baked beans from the fridge while the coffee brewed. She had sticks of sandalwood incense burning in several rooms, the aro-ma infiltrating the whole house, but it didn't help.

By midmorning, the shakes started. Michelle knew it wasn't from all the coffee she drank. Caffeine had so little effect on her these days. She turned on the TV and watched that for a while, but didn't even know what she was watching. She felt like an emotional wreck and she couldn't think straight.

By noon, she couldn't take it anymore. As the tears started welling, she climbed up the stairs, through the bedroom and into the closet. She pulled out her sock drawer and reached behind them, drawing out a small hinged box. She looked at it for a few moments, wishing she was stronger. Then, she wiped away a tear and went into the bathroom.

Within a couple of minutes, she had two lines laid out on the granite countertop. She picked up the short plastic straw from the box and, brushing away more disappointed tears, snorted a line up each nostril.

The effect was almost instantaneous. She felt the familiar numbness in her nostrils. As the coke was quickly absorbed through her mucous membranes and into her bloodstream, her brain began releasing dopamine. As her heart speeded up, the dopamine was rapidly pumped throughout her body. She sighed as she felt the euphoria wash over her. Suddenly, she felt better about herself, and the tears stopped.

She knew she had been needy and bitchy with Mark, and she wanted to make it up to him. And now, she felt as if she could. Gone was the depression, replaced by an energetic motivation to do something constructive.

She decided that it was time to get dressed.

§

By the time Mark got home, the flurry of activity had died down. The house smelled delicious, the table set for dinner, but Michelle was spent.

The effects of the cocaine had expired, and Michelle had moved on to Scotch.

"Oh my god," Mark said as he came through the arched doorway into the dining room, "it smells wonderful in here."

Michelle greeted him with a kiss, draping an arm around his neck. She could barely hold herself up.

"Welcome home, love," she said, squinting up at him. Even as blurry as he looked right now, she could still tell how good-looking he was.

"What's going on?" he asked.

"What do you mean?" Michelle asked, noticing that her pronunciation seemed to be a little off. She spoke a little more slowly and deliberately, concentrating on not slurring when she continued. "I treated you like shit this morning. I wanted to make you a nice dinner to make it up to you."

Through the haze, she thought she saw disappointment on Mark's face.

"I know you said you'd take me out to dinner," Michelle continued, "but I thought it'd be better if we had our dinner right here." Her face twisted into a lascivious grin. "Then we could just slip up to the bedroom and rip each other's clothes off." She looked behind her at the dining room table. "Or, we could sweep everything off the table and you could just fuck me there." Looking at the table, she snickered. "Although, come to think of it, it could be fun to do that in a restaurant, too."

Mark turned her around and walked her into the living room toward the sofa, supporting her with an arm around her back. Michelle smiled, remembering the times they had made love on the sofa. She had her blouse unbuttoned by the time he turned her around and sat her down. It flew open, revealing that she wasn't wearing a bra.

Michelle looked up at Mark while seductively circling her nipple with her fingertip. He stood there looking down at her, but Michelle couldn't understand why he didn't rip her clothes the rest of the way off. Then, it occurred to her: he was waiting for her. With an effort, she leaned forward and grabbed his belt, cupping his genitals in her other hand.

"Michelle, stop!" Mark demanded, stepping back out of her reach. She fell back on the sofa and squinted up at Mark as he hastily yanked the drapes closed.

"Honey, what's wrong?" she asked. Then, she gasped. "Didn't your meeting work out?" she asked sympathetically.

Mark looked down at her, his hands clenched together on top of his head. Michelle couldn't figure out his expression. He seemed upset.

"The meeting went fine," he replied. Michelle could hear the tension in his voice, though, and decided that he wasn't telling her the truth.

"Then why are you so –" She gasped again as she had a realization. "You're trying to spare me." Her eyes filled with tears. "You're so sweet to me. Baby, you can tell me if . . . it didn't turn out . . . very good."

Mark turned and started pacing back and forth across the living room, his hands still on his head, pulling nervously at his hair. Michelle wished he would hurry and spill it. She was so goddamned tired.

It was still early. Maybe she should take a nap before dinner. Then she'd be even more ready for a damn good fucking.

Maybe a nap would do Mark some good, too.

§

She opened her eyes and was surprised to find herself in bed. She didn't remember coming in here, though. The room was dark, and she was alone. Her mouth tasted like dirty socks, and her head was pounding. She turned to look at the clock, getting another good throbbing for the effort, and saw that it was nearly 1:30. The disorientation persisted, but since the room was dark, she decided that it was 1:30 in the morning.

She laboriously sat up and allowed her bare feet to drop to the plush rug beside her bed. With a groan, she stood up and dragged her feet toward the door, but before she got there, she felt her stomach protesting. She made a sudden beeline for the bathroom.

As she crouched over the toilet, her stomach purging, she knew she had fucked up. Fragments of memories of the day before flickered through her head.

One of those memories was Mark's look of disappointment.

She took a couple of minutes to brush her teeth, then she cautiously opened the bedroom door. All was silent. She padded quietly down the stairs into the living room where she found Mark sitting on the sofa, his back to her, his head in his hands.

She had the presence of mind to know that a breezy "Hey, babe, what are you doing up?" wouldn't go over very well. She walked quietly in and sat down in the wing-back chair across from Mark. Mark looked at her but remained silent. Michelle couldn't tell from his expression what he was thinking, and she realized that she was scared. Finally, he shook his head almost imperceptibly and took a breath.

"I'm sorry I wasn't around today," he said.

Michelle felt the air rush out of her lungs in a guilt-ridden gasp. She had steeled herself for a tongue lashing at the very least. An apology from Mark was the last thing she expected, and she felt her heart go out to him more than ever.

"What?" was all she could manage to say, her face twisted in confusion.

"I told you I'd be here for you, to help you with this. Today was obviously a tough day, and I just left you."

"No," Michelle replied, shaking her head. It felt good to not be the one making excuses for her behavior, but she felt bad letting Mark think he was to blame. She was entirely unaccustomed to that. "This wasn't your fault. This is totally on me." She noticed that Mark didn't contradict her, though, and she had a fleeting thought that he had used reverse psychology on her. But she had already begun her argument, and she believed in it. She continued on that tack.

"I wanted you to fuck me this morning," she continued, "and then I found out that you were leaving. I acted like a child. I couldn't handle it, and I gave in to the old cravings." She felt a surprising surge of pride in taking responsibility for her actions.

"So, what should we do about it?" Mark asked.

Michelle couldn't help noticing the lack of blame or accusatory tone in his voice. But she didn't know how to respond. The idea of going into rehab always terrified her. Having heard horror stories of withdrawal, she felt even more squeamish about it than when she was coming down from the drugs. When she didn't respond, Mark spoke up again.

"Maybe we should start with getting rid of the drugs."

"Yeah," Michelle nodded, and she quickly stood up. She had to wait a moment until her stomach caught up with her, then she pulled herself up the stairs. She drew the box out of her sock drawer and, feeling a little trepidation, took it downstairs where Mark waited for her.

Mark lifted the lid and looked inside. The little plastic bag was the main thing he was concerned about. He took the bag and handed the box back to Michelle.

"Are you going to flush it down the toilet?" she asked.

"I don't think so," he said, as he stood there thinking. "I'm not sure if waste-water treatment plants are equipped for this.

Not that there's that much here, but still, . . ." Finally, he seemed to have a plan. With the little bag clutched in his hand, he walked purposefully through the dining room, into the kitchen and pulled the trash can out from under the sink.

Michelle noticed that Mark had cleaned up the kitchen and put away the dinner she had prepared, and tears filled her eyes again at his thoughtfulness, and at the thought of having disappointed him. The trash can was still full of wet vegetable trimmings and other things that were starting to smell. The trash needed to go out.

She experienced a feeling of anxiety when Mark opened the bag and dumped the white powder into the mess in the trash can. He shook it around a little, then dropped the empty bag into it. Pulling up the edges of the trash bag, he tied up the top and pulled it out of the can.

He looked at her and smiled. Michelle's reaction was to burst into tears. Mark used his free hand and pulled her to him, holding her tightly.

"Hey," he said softly into her ear, "we'll get through this."

Michelle felt grateful for Mark's eagerness to help, but she wondered if his optimism was simply naivety.

13

Michelle was shivering, but sweat was pouring down her face. She could feel it soaking her clothing, dripping into her eyes. Mark was sitting on the edge of the bed beside her, his hand resting on her arm. He had lit a stick of incense for her, and it had nearly burned down to the holder on the headboard, but it wasn't making a dent in her anxiety.

Having sold Peer, Mark hadn't decided what his next venture would be yet. After coming home to Michelle's 'lapse' as he called it, he decided to take whatever time was necessary to get her clean. She was insistent about not going to a rehab center, so Mark did some research and determined that he would handle it, and he wouldn't leave the house until it was over.

Michelle was immensely appreciative when he told her. Now, she wanted to kill him.

She had made arrangements with the salon to take two weeks off. The depression that she had felt on Sunday morning returned with a vengeance, and she spent most of the first day just sleeping. It didn't matter how much she slept, though. She woke feeling fatigued and with a raging headache, along with guilt over being so weak and worthless.

There were fleeting moments when she realized how much Mark had done for her, preparing meals, making her drink plenty of water, just being supportive. But then the dark moods would descend again and engulf her.

Her homicidal thoughts about Mark subsided a bit as she fell asleep again.

By Friday, she started feeling a little better. The depression was still there, but Mark made it a point to be with her to help her through it. She felt as if she couldn't get enough to eat, and Mark brought her whatever she wanted, though after a day or so, he started bringing her smaller portions than she would have chosen for herself.

By that weekend, she was feeling better, as if she really could get over her need for the coke. Though the nights were bad. She could sleep, but her sleep was filled with nightmares. Mark was always on hand, though, to hold her and calm her fears after she woke up.

By the following week, she felt the old craving returning.

§

"Please," she begged, "I just need a bump to take the edge off." Mark sat on the sofa, a frown on his face.

"I don't know what a bump is," he replied, "but if it has anything to do with drugs, then you can fuggedaboudit." His attempt to lighten the mood didn't help.

"Mark," Michelle sobbed, "I can't do this."

"Yes, you can, Chelle. You're strong, and I'm here to help."

"I know, honey, but I'm not as strong as you think." She got up and knelt in front of him, her hands on his knees. "Please?"

"Sweetie, I have faith in you," Mark replied calmly but emphatically. "You can do this."

"I don't think quitting cold turkey is good for you," Michelle said with a reasoning tone. "Even rehab centers ease you off of it."

"They don't give you bumps *of cocaine."*

"No, but they use other drugs to make the withdrawal easier."

"You want to go to a rehab center?"

"No," Michelle replied, frustrated. Suddenly, she brightened as she recalled a potential bargaining chip. "I'll give you a blow job," she said hopefully, as she moved her right hand to grasp his penis through his pants. "I know you love that."

"I do," he replied calmly, pushing her hand away and placing his hands on her cheeks, "and if you still want to do that later, I'll definitely be onboard. But you're not getting any coke."

"God damn you fucking son of a bitch!" she spat, pushing herself up against his knees. Standing in front of him now, looking down at him, the anger passed quickly and turned back into desperate sobbing.

"I'm sorry, Mark" she cried, shaking her head back and forth vigorously as the tears left jagged tracks down her face. "I didn't mean that."

67

Mark stood up and put his arms around her. She started to push away, but he held her tightly, rocking her gently from side to side. Michelle calmed a little as she allowed herself to relax into that rhythm. She felt as if she was going crazy, as the moods roiled and shifted, usually dark, but never settling on just one for very long.

§

Michelle felt safe and secure, and loved, as she basked in Mark's embrace. It was Sunday morning, and he was still asleep against her back, his arm wrapped around her. Michelle felt as if she never wanted to move, snuggled up against him in a perfect, comforting spooning position.

The last couple of weeks had been grueling, but Mark, true to his word, never left her side. He had stayed here with her, and was strong when she wasn't. And now, she was clean. She could scarcely believe how clear her mind was. It felt so good. She would still have to be vigilant to not give in when temptations arose, but she felt as if she had turned a major corner.

As she lay there, warm under the covers, nestled in Mark's embrace, she pondered what she wanted to do that day. She wanted to be productive, and for the first time in quite a long time, she actually felt as if she could be.

Something with Mark, she thought. She owed him so much, and she wanted to show her appreciation to him. She remembered when she was bargaining with him almost a week ago to let her have a little coke, and the offer she had made then. A blow job, and everything that went with it, would certainly be nice, but she wanted to do something deeper, more meaningful than that.

Then, she realized that Christmas was just a couple of weeks away. What could be more meaningful than setting up the tree and decorating it together? Establishing a tradition that she could see stretching out for decades ahead of them.

She smiled as she thought of the two of them, old and grey, decorating the tree with ornaments they had gathered in their years together.

She felt Mark stir against her back, and she turned over to face him, inches away.

"Morning," he mumbled.

"Morning yourself," she smiled back. For a moment, she thought about the Christmas tree. But it was too early for that. They still had the whole day ahead of them.

Still smiling, she slipped beneath the covers, following Mark's body down into the warm darkness, tugging his shorts down.

14

Fin had pretty much stayed quiet while the opposing legal teams squared off against each other. Universal's lawyers were, obviously, well-versed in the legal issues and precedents, and they had a ready response for anything Intrepid threw their way. Fin felt he had nothing to add.

Besides, he was a little scared of Randall Black.

"This is a clear case of fan fiction," Jeremy Dyson said, his voice sounding a bit lower, as if he was trying to muster a little mettle. "Like your own film, *Fifty Shades of Grey*, was fan fiction of the *Twilight* series."

"Well, you're right about that, Mr. Dyson," Black replied with an easy smile, drawing on his extensive movie knowledge. "*Fifty Shades* started out as fan fiction when Ms. James first wrote it. But before she published it, you might say she filed off the serial numbers. She removed any and all references to *Twilight*. *Fifty Shades* bears little to no resemblance to the original work, so that now, people have to look up online to find out how the two are even related."

"Okay, so now I'd like to direct your attention," Dyson said, starting to sound a little cocky, "to the fact that *Call of the Dragon* is not the same as *DragonCache*. The characters are different, the situations are different –"

"The names have been changed to protect the guilty," Black interrupted, laughing, the other Universal lawyers joining in. "I'm afraid it don't work that way, son. Changing the names and a few situational details don't make the work yours."

"It happens all the time," John Whitson said, breaking his longtime silence. "Look at *Armageddon* and *Deep Impact*. If you read the description of each one of those films, you wouldn't be able to determine which movie was being referenced."

"That's true," Black replied. "That's because ideas can't be copyrighted." He chuckled. "Can you imagine some poor bonehead pitchin' his idea for a blockbuster disaster movie to a studio? They don't buy it, though, so he goes to another studio to pitch his idea. Well, they don't buy it either, and he leaves with his tail between his legs thinkin' what a loser he is and that he just can't come up with any good ideas.

"But there's no copyright on the idea, and now that idea's been planted in two different places. And despite what they told the poor fool that pitched it, they both decide they like it. That idea starts growin', but they develop it in completely different ways, with different characters and different plot points. The basic premise is identical, but they're two wildly different stories, one an action movie, the other character-driven." Randall Black smiled. "I don't know if that's how it happened with those two movies, but it happens all the time."

"So, how is that any different from our case?" Whitson asked. Dyson fidgeted a little as if he knew the answer, and Fin thought he might be wishing that Whitson would stop talking.

"Well," Black said, "let's have a look, shall we?"

He opened the screenplay to the first page and placed it in front of himself on the table. Then, he pulled a well-worn paperback copy of *DragonCache* from his briefcase, colored Post-it tabs sticking out all over, and opened it several pages in where some markings had been made, evidently referring to passages in the script.

"Here on the first page of your script, we're introduced to a young farm boy named Volano, whose father's killed by a dragon. Volano takes it upon 'imself to avenge 'is father and protect 'is village by trackin' down the dragon and killin' 'im.

71

"And here in *DragonCache*, we find Bodrun, a young farm boy whose father got himself killed by a dragon. Bodrun's pretty pissed off and takes it upon 'imself to avenge 'is father and protect 'is village by trackin' down and killin' the dragon."

"Okay," Whitson said belligerently, "that's the idea, the part you said couldn't be copyrighted. Farm boys going on quests are fairly common in movies. Like *The Princess Bride*. The difference is in the details. In *DragonCache*, Bodrun had brothers and sisters. In *Call of the Dragon*," he raised his eyebrows in a victorious expression, "Volano is an only child."

"Also a pretty common thing in movies," Black replied easily. "If you were making a series, you might leave those extra characters in there. But a two hour movie doesn't have time to explore the lives of too many side characters, so they get eliminated in the screenplay. Hell, they did it all the way back in *Gone With the Wind*. In the book, Scarlett O'Hara had a son by 'er first husband, Charles Hamilton and a daughter by 'er second husband, Frank Kennedy. In the movie, they eliminated both of 'em and she only had Bonnie Blue by rakish Rhett Butler."

Fin noticed that Dyson shot a pointed glance at Whitson, and Whitson seemed to back down then.

Black went through a few more obvious similarities between *DragonCache* and *Call of the Dragon* before he seemed to notice that the three from Intrepid Studios looked a little beaten down.

"Y'all look a little weary," he said, and again, Fin couldn't tell for certain if the concern was genuine or if he was being a sarcastic asshole. "Why don't we call it a day? We can meet back here tomorrow and pick up where we left off."

The three from Intrepid seemed eager to call it a day, though their faces fell a bit with the thought of resuming the torture the next day. Fin hadn't done anything but sit there and witness it all, and *he* was anxious to get out of there, as well.

15

W hat in the name of holy Saint freakin' Francis is this?" Mark asked. Michelle looked at him and at the ornament in his hand. She stood up straight and faced him directly, her hands on her hips.

"That's Falkor," she replied, with an indignant tone of voice. "Don't tell me you never saw The Neverending Story."

"I think I would remember seeing this," Mark replied, looking at the bizarre white dog-like creature in his hand.

"He's a luck dragon," Michelle said, taking the ornament from him and hanging it lovingly on the tree. "Many were the days I wished I had a luck dragon of my own," she said wistfully.

"Okay, princess," Mark replied. "I'm sorry I offended you."

Michelle looked up at Mark and smiled.

"You didn't offend me." She went back to pulling other ornaments out of the box. "But shit," she added under her breath, "who hasn't seen Neverending Story?"

She was surprised when she felt Mark's arms around her, pulling her up against him.

"Hey, Chelle, I'm sorry I made fun of your chupacabra."

"Falkor!" she corrected.

"Falkor, chupacabra, I knew it was something like that."

Giggling, Michelle twisted around until she was facing him, his arms still wrapped around her. She gazed into his eyes for a few seconds, the smile never leaving her face. Finally, she sighed and shook her head.

"I love you," she said, and immediately wished she could take it back when she saw the look on Mark's face.

"Whoa," he exclaimed. "That was a surprise."

The more Michelle thought about it, though, the more sure she was.

"Yeah," she breathed, "it was for me, too."

§

"Why don't you ever talk about your family?" Mark asked as they lay in bed. He had been reading, his head propped up against his pillows, and he hadn't turned his light off yet.

"Uh, well," Michelle stammered, feeling a little uncomfortable, "you already met my brother."

"Oh yes," Mark nodded. "Nicky." There were a few moments of silence. "Any other siblings?"

"No, just Nicky and me." She felt the discomfort growing.

"What about your parents?"

"Well shit, Mark, what about your parents? I haven't seen them around here."

"Hey, take it easy," Mark said, pushing himself up to sit back against the headboard. "I've told you my folks are in Florida. They come up here now and then for a visit, and I go down there periodically."

Michelle looked up at Mark and sighed as she pulled herself up to sit next to him.

"I'm sorry. I'm just not on good terms with my mother." Several more moments passed quietly. "Would you believe out of my whole family, I'm the well-adjusted one?" Mark smiled sympathetically.

"What does she do?" he asked.

"Last I heard, she was a nursing assistant at an assisted living facility."

"Really? That's kind of impressive, isn't it?"

"Is it? I mean she doesn't have a degree. You don't need one to be a nursing assistant." She looked down at her hands for a moment. "I remember hearing that she tried a couple of times to start the schooling to be a nurse, but she either flunked out or quit. That was when my father was still around and she had access to a little more money. But as far as I know, that's what she's always done. Different nursing homes, but the same job.

"My father left when I was four and Nicky was three. I don't know why for sure. Mom never talked about him, except to call him 'that motherfuckin' dickhead.'

"She was kind of a mess. Although to be fair," she added in a tone of voice that sounded as if she were being coerced, "I don't

75

know if she was a mess before my father left, or if that's what did it to her. Or maybe that's why he left. I think he left her with a lot of debt, too. Life was pretty hard. We always lived in a shitty place. Every one of them was a little worse than the last.

"The whole time we were growing up, my mother always wanted recognition for everything she was doing for us. When Nicky or I misbehaved, she'd turn on the tears. She'd go on and on about how we just don't appreciate her and all the sacrifices she was making for us. She was critical of every fucking thing I did. Nothing I ever did would please that woman. It was pretty much the same for Nicky."

She screwed up her face and looked up at Mark.

"To be honest, I don't really remember a lot of details. I was probably either stoned or I blocked them out.

"My wild years really started about the time I got into high school. If someone invited me to a party or anything else, I didn't care what it was, I went. I just had to get out of the house and away from her. I felt bad about leaving Nicky there with her. But I think he actually started doing the same thing around the same time.

"I turned eighteen a month after I graduated from high school, and I moved out. Three friends of mine from school got an apartment. It wasn't any better than the one I moved out of, but it was ours. And it was away from our parents."

"With a start like that," Mark said, a little amazed, "how did you become a cosmetologist and buy a house?"

"Hard work and amphetamines." She smiled bitterly. "And whatever aid was offered. The community college had a low-income incentive I was able to take advantage of, so I took a cosmetology course. Then, when I started making some money, I found a bank that approved a loan so I could buy this little Cape Cod. I know it's really small, but it's mine."

"Chelle, it's perfect," Mark said, looking around. "You've made a very nice, comfortable home here." He turned and looked at Michelle. "I happen to think you're pretty amazing. You've made a better life for yourself than a lot of people who actually have a support system."

Michelle felt engulfed in warmth with his compliment, and it brought tears to her eyes.

"Thank you." She leaned against his shoulder, and Mark responded by putting his arm around her. "That's why I feel like I need to give to people less fortunate than me. I used to be right down there in the gutter with them." She looked up at Mark.

"Not bad for a stoner chick, huh?"

"Not bad at all," Mark agreed with a chuckle. "And now, you've even kicked that."

"Thanks to you."

"I'll bet your mother would be proud of you, too."

"Aw shit, you just had to go and spoil it."

"I'm not saying you need to make her a part of your life. But think of the guilt and regret you'd feel if something happened to her."

"Guilt and regret?"

"I know she was a shitty mother," Mark conceded, "but you know what? I've come to the conclusion that we all do the best we can manage under our particular circumstances. She wasn't great, by any means, but she was probably the best mother she could be with the cards she was dealt."

Michelle pondered that thought for a moment. She had already admitted that her mother was left with some difficulties. And she and Nicky hadn't exactly helped the situation. She looked up at Mark, hoping that he might give her an out, some reason to not go through with it. But she had already learned that Mark didn't work that way. Finally, she sighed.

"Okay, I'll give her a call."

Mark smiled.

"See," he said with conviction, "you're not afraid to try something just because it's difficult." He kissed her on the tip of her nose. "That's why I love you."

Then he turned, switched off his lamp and scooted down under the covers, but Michelle saw the mischievous smile on his face as he did so. He loved her. She felt as if her heart did a flip in her chest, but she didn't want to risk spoiling the moment. She slipped down under the covers herself, snuggling up against his back, and she fell asleep clutching him tightly.

§

Suzy sat still in the wing-back chair, unable to move. Her head lay back, resting against one of the wings, her arms dangling down both sides as if they were too heavy to lift. Her eyes gazed across the room into the corner where the Christmas tree had stood in the earlier episode, as her eyes filled with tears, and she smelled a brief whiff of sandalwood.

She was having a hard time living up to her earlier resolve to leave herself out of it, to just pay attention to Michelle and whatever her unfinished business might be. She remembered the feeling of Mark's body pressed against her body in bed, her arms around him. *I know, I know, it was Michelle's body and Michelle's arms.* But that didn't lessen the physical and emotional reaction it engendered in Suzy.

And there was something bothering her about the episodes themselves, something she couldn't quite place yet.

Sunshine poured in through the window next to the chair, bathing Suzy in warmth, replacing the warmth that she had felt from Mark's body. As she drifted off into an uneasy sleep, she had a wavering impression of Michelle watching her from the foot of the stairs.

16

Rachel sat open-mouthed as Suzy, pale-faced and wooden as if she were in complete shock, related a few details of the episodes she had been experiencing. When Suzy stopped talking, Rachel was still silent.

Back in Michelle's house, Suzy had woken from her unexpected nap in the wing-back chair, confused and a little disoriented. Unexpectedly, a creepy old rhyme from her childhood appeared in her head.

> The other day upon the stair,
> I saw a man that wasn't there.
> He wasn't there again today.
> I wish that man would go away.

Remembering, she looked toward the stairs where she thought she had seen Michelle earlier, before the episode began, but there was nobody there. Not now, anyway. She figured she had probably just dreamed that Michelle was there watching her. Despite the warmth of sitting next to the window, Suzy had shivered.

It was nearly 4:00. She didn't know when Joan would be home, but she didn't want to see her or talk to her. The whole situation was just too awkward. She knew Joan would ask her how it was going, and Suzy didn't know what she could possibly tell her. The truth was out of the question.

She found a piece of paper in her purse and dashed off a quick note, letting Joan know that it was going well and that she would be back in the morning. She knew Joan wouldn't be satisfied with that, but she hoped she could think of something to tell her by then.

She needed to talk to someone, though, and she knew it couldn't be Joan. It *really* couldn't be Fin. So she called her best friend, Rachel, who was on her way home from work. Rachel invited Suzy to meet her at her house. Rachel poured a couple of glasses of chardonnay, and they sat on the sofa in her living room.

"So, it's like you're actually *with* Mark?" Rachel finally asked quietly. "You're conversing with him and . . ." she lowered her voice, "making love to him."

"It's *exactly* like that," Suzy replied, still in a daze. "Well," she corrected, "no, not exactly. They're not my thoughts or my actions. I don't have any influence over what is said or done. You know, I don't initiate the actions. But I feel it. I experience it. It's just that someone else is composing the script.

"Shit," Rachel replied under her breath. "Does Fin know about this?"

"I can't tell Fin about this," Suzy insisted, with more spirit than she had been able to muster before.

Rachel nodded her head knowingly, but she raised her eyebrows at Suzy.

"Don't you think he's going to ask?"

"He already did," Suzy replied. "Last night. I basically blew him off with a remark about Michelle being such a mess. Which is true, except . . ." Suzy looked away, distracted, pondering.

"Except what?"

"She actually got off the drugs." Suzy pulled her attention back to Rachel. "Thanks to Mark. I never knew that. I just thought Michelle was always a wild party girl. I never knew she wanted to be anything different, and that she actually succeeded at some point."

"Mark never talked about her?"

"No. I mean a comment once in a great while, if it was on topic, but neither of us ever really made it a practice to discuss our previous relationships." She took a sip of her wine, then looked sharply at Rachel. "I just realized what was bothering me."

"What?" Rachel replied. "You're channeling the ghost of a dead friend and reliving her romance with her ex, who happens to be your late husband, and something's bothering you about it?"

"Hey," Suzy said with a hint of a smile, "*I'm* supposed to be the smartass in this outfit."

"You seemed a little off your game today," Rachel said wryly. "I'm just filling in."

"That was good," Suzy conceded. Then, her face resumed its serious expression.

"Michelle was a wild, gregarious, drug-addicted, life-of-the-party. I'm a laid-back introvert whose idea of a perfect Friday night is a pizza, a glass of wine and a good book. What the hell did Mark see in me?"

"Are you kidding?" Rachel exclaimed. "You're more like Mark was than anybody I've ever known. And you're beautiful, and funny, and smart. I could just as easily ask, 'What the hell did he see in Michelle?'"

"Well, thank you. But Michelle was beautiful, too. And obviously driven. And apparently smart enough to be a successful businesswoman, even despite the drugs and alcohol."

"Admirable qualities. And apparently Mark was deep enough to see through Michelle's shallow party-girl exterior to appreciate those traits.

"With you, though, he didn't have to dig through all that shit and look for your good qualities. They weren't hidden behind a crazy drug and alcohol-induce veneer. They're just who you are. After Michelle, you were probably an immense relief."

"I suppose," Suzy acknowledged, though she didn't sound completely convinced. She sighed. "I just never knew it was that serious. He told her he loved her. I always thought she was just an old girlfriend."

"Well, whatever he felt for her," Rachel said, "it wasn't enough to keep him there. He married you."

"I just can't figure out why I'm there. Obviously, there's something holding her here."

"Can't you just tell her to go into the light? I mean isn't that what you say? Go into the light? Go through the door? Something like that?"

"I don't know. I mean I've done that on a couple of occasions in the past, but it's pretty rare. I think this is just a lot more complex. Michelle specifically asked her mother to call me. How many times have you heard of a ghost asking for that?"

"That *is* pretty freaky," Rachel agreed.

"And this is so big on an emotional level for me," she said, burying her face in her hands. "How can I possibly keep something this monumental from my fiancé?"

"Wait, what? Your fiancé?"

Suzy looked up at her and smiled sheepishly.

"Oh, yeah."

§

"Oh my god, it was brutal!" Fin said. Suzy, at home now, sat perched on her sofa looking out over the bay, her phone pressed to her ear. Ursula was curled up next to her on the sofa. "These guys really don't know what they're up against. Or at least they didn't. They're learning pretty quickly."

"Do you think it'll be wrapped up tomorrow?" Suzy asked.

"I honestly have no idea. I don't know anything about how long this kind of thing usually takes to play out. For Intrepid's sake, I hope it's over soon."

"Yeah," Suzy replied absently.

"How's Ursula doing?"

"She's fine," Suzy said, petting the dog. "She spent the whole day alone in the backyard, so she's been sticking close to me since I got home."

Fin had enclosed a sizable portion of the backyard, including the carriage house where Suzy had discovered her first ghost, Fiona, her great-great-great-great-great-grandmother. After placing a comfy dog bed and a bowl of water in a sheltered area, they felt more comfortable when they had to leave the dog alone.

"So, how was your day? Did you get Michelle sent off?"

"No, not yet. Like I said last night, she was such a mess. It's just hard getting through the episodes." The guilt pounded down on her again. The statement was absolutely truthful, but still misleading. "And I haven't been able to determine yet what's holding her here, what her unfinished business is."

"Well, you're the smartest and bravest and strongest woman I've ever known," Fin said, making Suzy lower her head in shame. She was glad Fin couldn't see her. "I know you'll figure it out."

"God, I wish I had your faith in me."

"Hey, that doesn't sound like my favorite smartass."

"Yeah, I seem to be getting that a lot lately." She sighed. "I'll get it back. I just need to get through this case."

17

The air was thick with sandalwood the next morning, and Joan looked even worse when Suzy showed up at her door. Her eyelids seemed too heavy to raise more than halfway. What little Suzy could see of them, it was difficult to see where the bloodshot whites ended, and the brown irises began.

"Are you making any progress at all?" Joan asked, her voice a little shaky.

"It's hard to say," Suzy replied sympathetically. "I'm just not sure yet what it is Michelle's trying to tell me." Joan sighed as Suzy dropped her purse beside the wing-back chair. "Do you mind if I ask what it is that Michelle's doing? I mean, what is it like here at night?"

Joan shook her head and opened her mouth, then closed it again as she tried to gather her thoughts. She shook her head again and looked at Suzy.

"A lot of screaming. Yelling at me, blaming me for her shitty life." She quickly put her hand up to her mouth. "Sorry. I don't usually talk like that. I just . . . I don't think I've slept more than two or three hours in the last several nights."

"Is there somewhere else you can stay for a night or two?" Suzy asked as a thought occurred to her. "I'll really focus on powering through this, and maybe I can even stay overnight. But a lot of it depends on Michelle and being able to clear up her unfinished business with me."

Joan looked at Suzy through bleary eyes.

"You told me a couple of days ago that these episodes, as you call them, are like you're there in Michelle's life. Is that right?"

"Yes, it's as if I *am* Michelle. I'm seeing her memories through her eyes."

"But you can't just skip over that and convince her to go into the light?"

"Not if there's something powerful holding her here. I need to know what it is and possibly help her with it. But if I can just concentrate on getting through however many episodes she wants to show me, even into the night, if necessary, maybe I can help her get it resolved and she can move on.

"Do you have a friend you can stay with?" Suzy asked again.

"Yeah, maybe," Joan replied. She glanced around as if undecided. As she stood there wavering, Suzy spoke up again, trying to help her along.

"If you have a few minutes before you have to leave for work, why don't you pack a bag and call a friend. After you leave, I'll get started, and I'll try to keep at it uninterrupted until it's done."

"Okay," Joan nodded, and she turned and wearily climbed the stairs.

Suzy gazed at the foot of the stairs where she thought she had seen Michelle the afternoon before, just before drifting off to sleep. She took in a long, uneasy breath as she pondered this strange interaction she had with dead people. Knowing that Michelle was still there somewhere, she glanced around, wondering what she would see today when the episodes began.

Again, she felt guilty. She had been deliberately misleading both Joan and Fin, not because of her desire to do the right thing with Michelle, but to be able to spend more time with Mark. She didn't like to think about how she would feel when the episodes ended.

A few minutes later, Joan came back downstairs with a bag in one hand and her phone in the other. She gathered up her purse and keys, and left an extra key for Suzy in case she needed to leave. "Call me if you need anything," she said sluggishly.

"I will, Joan," Suzy replied. "Thank you. I hope you can get some sleep tonight."

§

Michelle sat slumped in the wing-back chair, the official-looking sheet of paper dangling loosely in her hand. She felt lost and scared, her heart pounding in her chest as if she had been running for her life. Without the contents of her little box upstairs in her sock drawer, she didn't feel as if she had the strength to deal with it.

It didn't help that she had been feeling the sensation of someone watching her. Mark had told her that paranoia was a possible side effect of withdrawal, but it was pretty damn unsettling.

She had no idea how long she'd been sitting there. It had gotten dark since she sat down, but she felt unmotivated to get up and turn on a light. The only light in the room was from the streetlight across the street, and the colorful glow from the Christmas tree. She felt anything but merry.

Instead, she felt petrified, unable to move or make a decision. She barely even looked up when Mark walked in the door and turned the light on. He could see right away that something was wrong.

"Hey, what is it?" he asked, his voice heavy with concern. As an answer, she lifted her hand and held out the paper. Mark walked around the sofa and the coffee table and took the paper from her, glancing over it quickly.

"Foreclosure?" He looked at Michelle. "Why? What's going on?"

Michelle felt the tears welling up as she took a deep breath.

"I bought this house with something called a balloon mortgage. They told me I'd make regular payments for a few years, then when the balloon came due, I could refinance. The balloon payment came due, but that lender has gone out of business, and another bank now owns my loan."

"Hmm," Mark nodded. "I've been hearing about that a lot lately."

"I've lost count of how many banks I've gone to," Michelle continued as the tears slipped down her cheeks. "Nobody will

86

give me a loan, Mark. I can't refinance. They're going to take my house away from me."

Mark knelt down in front of Michelle, holding her hands in his.

"Nobody's taking your house."

"But –" Michelle protested, motioning toward the letter from the bank, but Mark shook his head.

"Don't worry, honey. I promise you nobody's going to take your house."

Mark leaned forward and took her in his arms, and she could feel the apprehension fade as he held her. It returned for a bit that night, affecting her sleep, renewing her cravings, but again, Mark's presence helped her to relax.

She was preparing dinner when he came home the following evening. After he hung up his coat in the closet, he came into the kitchen.

"Hi baby," Michelle said as she looked up at him. She noticed he had an odd expression on his face. She put down the knife and wiped her hands on a dish towel. She turned toward him, squinting at him. "What are you up to?"

Mark grinned and held up the foreclosure notice. Michelle's face fell when she was reminded, but Mark began tearing the notice into small pieces, then dropped them into the trash can under the sink. Michelle looked back up at Mark, a confused frown on her face.

"The house is yours," Mark said.

"I don't understand."

"I made the balloon payment. They stopped the foreclosure."

Michelle felt as if the breath was pulled from her lungs.

"You paid off my house?" she whispered.

"Well, I figured it benefited me, too, since I live here. It's too cold for me to be living on the street."

She felt the tears coming again, but no words would come. She felt rooted in place, so she was glad when Mark took a couple of steps toward her, and she fell into his arms. After at least a minute of crying into his chest and feeling the comforting caress of his hands on her back, she pulled away and looked up at him, drying her tears on the dish towel in her hands.

"You should receive the official papers in a few days," Mark concluded.

"I don't know what to say," she said in a whisper as the tears reassembled in formation on her lower lids.

"You don't have to say anything," Mark replied.

§

Mark stopped in front of a brick building that looked as if, in its better days, it had been a warehouse. Having fallen from that status decades ago, it had been divided into apartments, and then, apparently, forgotten. It was in a rough neighborhood in Roxbury, just southwest of Boston.

"Are you sure we're in the right place?" Michelle asked.

"That's what the GPS says," Mark replied. "The number over the door is correct. I think this is it."

"The address is different, but not much has changed," Michelle said quietly.

"You okay?" Mark asked. Michelle looked at him, her expression less than confident. She had taken a hit from her bong, of the last bit of grass she had, then a breath mint to hopefully hide it from Mark. It had helped, but her anxiety was returning now. After a brief delay, she smiled weakly and nodded.

Mark pulled into the parking lot next to the building and into an empty space. He shut off the engine and they both got out of the car. They each opened their respective back doors, and Michelle picked up a box from the back seat wrapped with red and green paper featuring holly leaves and berries. Mark picked up a box containing two covered dishes, one which held a salad, the other a pumpkin pie.

When Michelle, at Mark's suggestion, called her mother, Joan had been surprised to hear from her, but agreeable to meet. She invited them over for lunch on Christmas day. And now, that day had arrived.

Together, they approached the front door and looked at the panel covered with pieces of masking tape, each with a different name written on it. Michelle found Joan Rossi in apartment 3-10 and pressed the button next to it. A few seconds later, there was a raspy buzz, and she pulled the door open.

Inside the building, the light from outside couldn't penetrate very far beyond the grimy glass door. The entry was illuminated by a dirty 40 watt bulb, and they climbed to the third floor and found the apartment. They exchanged a look, Michelle's decidedly more jittery than Mark's, as Michelle sighed and knocked on the door.

The door was flung open, and they were greeted by a face that Michelle hadn't seen in several years.

"Oh, my baby girl," she said. She threw her arms around Michelle, and Michelle quickly moved the gift to the side to prevent it from being crushed. Her mother held her for what seemed to be an interminably long time. Michelle could smell wine on her stale breath. Her stomach felt as if it was doing flip-flops as the old tension returned. Joan finally released Michelle from the embrace and held her at arm's length, just looking at her, her eyes filled with tears.

She sighed, then turned and looked at Mark, letting go of Michelle. Michelle gave a sigh of relief. Her mother roughly wiped the tears from her eyes and smiled.

"You must be Mark. I'm Joan."

"Very nice to meet you, Joan," Mark replied with a warm smile.

"Please come in," Joan said. "Put that stuff down and make yourself at home."

Mark and Michelle entered the apartment, and Joan seemed embarrassed.

"It's not much, I'm afraid, but it's the best I can offer you," she said.

"Oh, please," Mark said graciously, "it's fine."

It was a small apartment, last renovated, it appeared, sometime in the seventies. The dining room was differentiated from the living room only by the presence of stained and, in places, gouged linoleum, and by the presence of the table and chairs.

The apartment was cluttered with years of stuff, in some places piled two feet high or more against the wall, old newspapers and magazines, boxes that were obviously empty because of being misshapen under the weight of the things stacked on top of them.

The stained and matted carpet was roughened in places where a vacuum cleaner had been pushed along the pathway.

Despite the aromas of the cooking food, Michelle detected the familiar odor, the smell of must and mold, and of spills that had never been wiped up and went stale, or that collected dust and bugs. She couldn't see them, but she knew they were there, probably under all the stuff. Mark was magnanimous enough that he didn't even seem to notice.

"I'm just so happy you're actually here," Joan effused as Michelle placed the gift next to a couple of others under the little tree in the living room. Michelle saw a nearly empty wine glass standing on an end table beside what had once been an over-stuffed chair.

Michelle didn't trust herself to make a response. The annoyance displayed on her face, though, expressed that her feelings were slightly less ecstatic. Mark jumped in to try to remedy the awkwardness.

"We're really glad we could come." As Joan directed him, he placed his dishes on a small clear area of a small countertop in the small galley kitchen.

"Can I take your coats?" Mark and Michelle shrugged out of their jackets, and Joan placed a hand on Mark's bicep. "It's crazy that you only needed these light jackets today. We should have had a white Christmas."

Michelle glared at Joan and her hand, but she managed to bite her tongue. Joan didn't seem to notice as she hung up the jackets in a small closet beside the door.

"Would you like some wine?" she asked.

"No, thank you," Mark replied, with a quick glance toward Michelle, "I think I'll pass." Joan looked at Michelle, and Michelle shook her head. She wasn't officially "on the wagon," but Mark had encouraged her to not use alcohol as a substitute for her craving for drugs. He had been abstaining for the last few weeks, for her sake, and with his support, Michelle had managed as well. She sure felt as if she could use a drink now, though.

"Okay. Uh, I have Scotch, bourbon, vodka, beer."

"Just water for me," Mark said.

"Me too," Michelle nodded, putting her hand through the crook of Mark's elbow.

"Huh," Joan said as if she didn't know what to make of it. "Okay." She turned and went into the kitchen and returned with two glasses of water.

"The ham should be done in a few minutes," she said, and she invited them to sit down in the living room. Mark and Michelle sat side by side on a worn love seat, while Joan sat opposite them in the chair. Michelle didn't notice when Joan had refilled her glass, but it was now full again.

The ensuing small talk felt uncomfortable to Michelle, and she thought her mother was uncomfortable, too. From small talk, the conversation progressed to embarrassing stories from Michelle's childhood. Some she wished she could forget, others she figured her brain must have blocked out.

It seemed to Michelle that Joan was overcompensating, being incredibly charming and amiable, probably hoping to disprove whatever horror stories she figured Michelle must have told Mark about her. She laughed frequently, usually at something Mark said, swirling her rapidly emptying wine glass in her hand. To Michelle's chagrin, Mark seemed to be buying Joan's ruse, apparently enraptured with her.

He seemed perfectly fine, though. He was so personable, visiting with Joan as if she were an old and dear friend. Michelle felt conflicted. She was happy that he took over the burden of keeping her mother engaged, but at the same time, Michelle was accustomed to being the life of the party. Not that spending time with her mother was a party, by any means, but still that odd internal discord was annoying. So, she was happy when the bell sounded in the kitchen, announcing that the ham was ready.

The sooner this fiasco was over, the better.

Mark and Michelle stood beside the table as Joan placed the ham in the center.

"Baby girl," Joan said, "could you help me bring the rest of the food out?"

"Mother, stop calling me 'baby girl'," Michelle demanded indignantly. "I'm not a baby."

"You'll always be my baby," Joan countered. "And I wish you would call me 'mom.' Why do you always insist on calling me 'mother'? It sounds so formal."

"'Mom' is too personal," Michelle said quietly. "'Mother' is strictly biological."

Joan cast a tearful glance at Mark, as if it was a silent exasperated plea. Mark looked at Michelle, an embarrassed expression on his face. The problem was Michelle didn't know for certain who he was embarrassed for. And she wasn't sure, but she thought there might have even been a bit of a reprimand in that look.

She narrowed her eyes as she pondered, then she sighed and went into the kitchen, grabbing a couple of the dishes of food. She placed them on the table, a little harder than she had planned, but the jarring noise accurately expressed her mood.

"Alright, young lady" Joan said, obviously miffed by now, "I agreed to this little get-together because you're my girl and I don't think families should be broken apart like we've been. But if you're going to act like this, then I don't see the point. I had hoped to get my daughter back. I don't want a huffy twelve-year-old."

"Fine," Michelle said, and she held her hand out to Mark. "Can I have the keys? I'll wait in the car."

"Michelle," Mark said, obviously uncomfortable himself by now. He cast a glance at Joan, then came up close to Michelle. He spoke in a quiet but firm voice. "Can you just try to be civil with her? It's going to take some hard work from both of you to overcome the last few years."

"The last few years?" Michelle echoed. "What about my life? That woman has made my life hell."

"Oh, please," Joan said, rolling her eyes disgustedly.

"Shut up, mother!" Michelle spat. "You've never taken any responsibility for all the shit you've pulled. Why do you think Nicky and I are both so fucked up?"

"You can't put that on me. You and those loser friends of yours were a mess when you were in high school, and you couldn't wait to get out from under my roof."

"I spent my childhood cleaning up your shit," Michelle retorted, gesturing to the piles of stuff. "I should have been outside playing with my friends, except that I usually didn't have any, because we had to move every six months. I helped you to bed every fucking time you passed out drunk in your chair. I cleaned up your puke and your piss, and when I was old enough and decided I couldn't take it anymore, then yes, I got the fuck away from you." She looked at Mark.

"And I'm sorry I let Mark talk me into coming back." She held her hand out toward Mark again. "Please?"

Mark looked at her for a moment, the anguish showing on his face, then he turned to Joan.

"Joan, I'm sorry. Maybe we should go. I guess I shouldn't have pushed this like I did."

"I appreciate you trying, Mark," Joan replied in an exasperated end-of-her-rope tone. Michelle almost expected her to follow it with a melodramatic 'What's a mother to do?' The tears were filling Joan's eyes again. "But you're right," she continued, "it's going to take both of us to make this work." She looked pointedly at Michelle, but Michelle ignored her, still looking at Mark.

Mark opened the closet door and pulled out their jackets, and Joan placed the salad and the pie back in the box that Mark had carried them in. As Michelle pulled her jacket on, Joan said, "I love you, honey."

"Fuck you," Michelle replied.

§

The drive home was quiet, but Mark apparently didn't want to just let it go. After they put the pie and the salad away in the kitchen, they took their jackets off and hung them up in the closet. Michelle turned toward the stairs, anxious to change into comfort clothes, but Mark grabbed her hand. She stopped and looked up at him.

"I'm sorry," he said. "I shouldn't have stuck my nose where it didn't belong. It was obviously too soon to ask something like this of you."

Michelle thought for a moment, still feeling the anger welled up inside her. God, she could sure use a little chemical help right

93

now! Maybe a hit from her bong would ease it a little, if she could coax any more out of it.

"Thank you," she replied shakily, her voice quiet and low. Her body quivered from the pent-up indignation. "I can't believe that bitch had the nerve to get mad at me. And to call me a huffy twelve-year-old."

Mark looked at her, an empathetic expression on his face. But he didn't respond. Michelle narrowed her eyes a bit.

"You don't agree with her, do you?" she asked.

"Well," he hesitated, "I wasn't there when you were growing up. All I have to go by is what was said. But I have to admit I can see both sides."

Michelle looked piercingly at him and the empathy on his face morphed into something else. Consternation? Foreboding?

"You can see how I was a huffy twelve-year-old?" Her voice had an icy edge to it.

"Honey," Mark replied carefully, "do you remember a few weeks ago when we first started getting you off the drugs? I shared with you a study that showed how drug use stunts the growth of certain parts of the brain having to do with emotional development. We knew that there would probably be issues involving adolescent maturation. We knew that you might experience impulsive behavior, mood swings –"

"So, you think I was being immature?" Michelle interrupted. "You agree with that fucking bitch?"

"Sweetheart," Mark started, but he didn't get any further.

"Don't 'sweetheart' me," she spat as she jerked her hand away. Deep down, she knew he was probably right about the mood swings, but she didn't feel as if she could reach that deep. It felt, instead, as if it was completely out of her control. At the moment, she didn't feel as if she could control anything.

She turned on her heel and stormed up the stairs. "You can sleep on the sofa tonight, asshole."

18

Suzy wasn't accustomed to feeling angry at Mark, especially not in the last few years since his death. But as she came out of the episode, she felt that residual anger as Michelle's feelings left their imprint on Suzy's consciousness.

It was quickly replaced with shame and remorse as she mentally asked Mark to forgive her for feeling that second-hand emotion.

Lethargically, she sat there in the wing-back chair, pondering what she had just experienced, and all the episodes she had experienced before. She wondered how much she was affected by the episodes, and by what Michelle felt.

Even as she sat there pondering, she had the feeling of someone watching her. She forced herself to turn her head to the left, to look out the window, but she didn't see anybody. She remembered Michelle's paranoia, thinking that someone was watching her, and figured it was probably just another instance of what Michelle experienced bleeding over into Suzy's consciousness, like her anger at Mark.

The conflicting feelings about Mark led, inevitably, to the conflicting feelings she had been feeling about Fin. She felt weighed down by the ever-present guilt that had been accompanying her thoughts of him. She knew she hadn't lied to him, but she had intentionally misled him. But how could she tell him the truth about the episodes? How could she tell him that the episodes dealt with Mark, and that Suzy was feeling him touch her, kiss her, make love to her?

She knew she couldn't, but she didn't know what to do. She had told Joan that she would continue with the episodes and help Michelle to move on, but she needed help with deciding what to do with her own feelings.

§

Lilith, Suzy's spirit expert and counselor, sat in her chair, her feet dangling, not quite touching the floor, and listened patiently as Suzy related what she had been experiencing over the last few days. Her iron-grey hair curled haphazardly around her face. Her gnarled hands were folded in her lap, her face serene and almost, but not quite, on the verge of a smile.

As Suzy spoke, she felt the tension ease. She didn't know if it was because of the easy, welcoming manner that Lilith displayed, or from the happily dancing flames of the candles that were burning throughout Lilith's dim living room. Or maybe the profusion of crystals lining the perimeter of practically every horizontal surface had some effect on her emotions. That sort of thing had always seemed a little too "woo-woo" for Suzy, but in the last few years, she had learned not to discount something just because it didn't go along with conventional wisdom.

Having finished relating the gist of the episodes, Suzy sat back and sighed.

"I just don't know how to handle this," she said. "Just when I feel strong enough to say yes to Fin's proposal, Mark is thrown back into my life again."

At that, Lilith's smile broke through.

"Well, dear, you do know it's not really Mark, don't you?"

"I do," Suzy nodded vigorously. "I know I'm just experiencing someone else's past memories of him. But it's real enough that I feel his touch, and I feel – those feelings. I know it's Michelle's experience of Mark, but I still feel it, and it's still Mark. And I feel it when I come out of it."

"And you feel guilty about still being attracted to him now that you've promised to marry your Fin."

"Yes," Suzy replied in a whisper.

"You told me a while back about how Mark died." Suzy felt the tension return at Lilith's mention of the incident, and she nodded. "You said that you felt guilty about it. Is that still the case?"

"Sure, when I let myself think about it. It was my fault. Not just because I was the one driving the boat, but also because he didn't want to go out in the first place. He wanted to stay home and make love, but I kept nagging him until he gave in. So, yeah, because of me, my husband and my little girl died." She reached up and impatiently wiped away a tear.

Lilith looked at Suzy for a few moments. Suzy was starting to feel uncomfortable under the old woman's intense gaze when Lilith finally responded.

"I wonder if that's the guilt that you're feeling now. Of course, engaging with your husband would be compelling. And it's certainly understandable that you feel as if you're being unfaithful to Fin by entertaining these feelings and experiences with Michelle's memories of Mark. But I think the deeper issue, the reason these experiences are having such a profound effect, is that you feel as if Mark hasn't forgiven you."

"Well, there is that," Suzy agreed with a sarcastic tone. "And that still pisses me off. I'm able to have all these interactions with these other dead people, but my own husband and daughter are out of my reach. How is that fair?"

"It's not," Lilith replied, shaking her head. "And I can't tell you why that is. But I think a reasonable possibility is that, since both your husband and your daughter passed on at the same time, Mark felt protective of Emma. He felt responsible for her, so rather than lingering here in the physical world, he stayed with her and accompanied her into the next realm."

"That makes sense," Suzy nodded. Then, she noticed a puzzling look come over Lilith's face. "What is it?"

Lilith pondered a moment before responding.

"A thought just occurred to me. Have you ever gone back out to the site of the accident?"

"No," Suzy replied, a look of near terror on her face.

"It's not unheard of," Lilith shrugged, "for a spirit to remain in the location of their death, even if that location is in the water. They no longer depend on physical conditions for their existence."

"Interesting," Suzy said slowly, her tone of voice adding an unspoken 'and a little creepy.'

"Especially might that be the case if there was a strong emotional connection to that location. Since Emma died there, too, it's possible that he, or they, remained there instead of going back to your house."

Suzy thought about it for a while. As a theory, it made sense. Suzy had experienced no further desire to go boating and had studiously stayed off the water since that day. But perhaps, with strong enough motivation, she might be able to manage one more outing.

"Mind you," Lilith said, "that's just a random thought I had. There's absolutely no guarantee that that's what happened. I think it's just as possible, in fact more so, that what I said earlier is what happened, that he guided Emma to the next plane."

"Of course," Suzy said, still trying to muster up the courage to visit the site of the accident.

"Regardless of whether that's the case or not," Lilith concluded softly, but firmly, "and even more important than your perception of Mark's forgiveness, is that *you* need to forgive *yourself*."

§

Suzy didn't know if that visit with Lilith helped or not. The thought about forgiving herself, well, it wasn't a new thought, but it was a less than welcome reminder. She recalled Rachel suggesting it a while back. But it certainly gave her something to think about as she drove back to Saugus and Michelle's house.

In fact, she was thinking seriously enough about it that she almost missed the fact that a grey Honda seemed to be following her. When she finally noticed that the car changed lanes the same time she did, again, her conversation with Lilith took a back seat.

She remembered her thoughts earlier about Michelle's paranoia bleeding into her own consciousness, so she tried not to panic. But she kept her eye on the Honda, about three cars back, as she turned right off Lynnway onto Blossom Street. Watching her rear-view mirror as the other cars passed, she saw the grey Honda make the turn.

Her heart was pounding now, and she didn't know why. What possible reason would anybody have for following her?

A few blocks later, as she approached the traffic light at Neptune Boulevard, the grey Honda slowed down, hanging farther back. The light turned green as she approached it, and she turned left. Going slower than she should have, she watched her mirror and saw the grey Honda turn left as well.

Struggling to keep her breathing slow and steady, Suzy veered off to the right a block later onto Summer Street. She didn't know whether to keep driving slowly, to try to get a glimpse of the driver in her mirror, or if she should speed up and try to lose them.

The situation resolved itself when she saw the grey Honda continue straight on Neptune instead of following her onto Summer. She pulled over under the shade of a large elm tree and leaned her head forward on the steering wheel, as her breathing gradually resumed a more normal pattern.

19

The people from Intrepid Studios seemed to have lost most of whatever steam they might have had the previous day. Jeremy Dyson sat forward, perhaps trying to regain some of that steam, leaning against the table, while Whitson sat back in his chair, mouth clamped shut. Fin wondered if Dyson had impressed on him the need for him to let his lawyer do the talking.

Only one of the Universal executives was back today, since the legal team was left fully in charge of the proceedings.

"I appreciate the time you took yesterday," Dyson started after taking a deep, cleansing breath, "explaining the intricacies of fan fiction. The three of us spent a good deal of time last night discussing that, and other things, and we've reached a somewhat different conclusion. We really think that this is more a case of 'derivative work' versus 'transformative work.'"

From his seat, Fin noticed that Randall Black raised his head a bit, leading with his chin, as if he was ready to engage, but he remained quiet while Dyson continued. Fin also noticed that Dyson hesitated as if he had noticed that gesture as well.

"Intrepid's screenplay for *Call of the Dragon* may bear certain similarities to *DragonCache*, but those similarities are not enough to make it a derivative work." He glanced down at his notes, and Fin got the impression he has having trouble believing it himself. Out the corner of his eye, Fin saw Randall Black smile. "*Call of the Dragon* has been altered enough from *DragonCache* that we feel it would be considered a transformative work."

"Well, that's an interesting point," Black said. "But I might recommend that, when arguin' your case before the judge, you refrain from using the word 'altered.' You're just drawin' attention to the fact that *DragonCache* was the original work that you used to create your script."

Fin saw Dyson's Adam's apple rise and fall as he swallowed nervously, and he wondered if Dyson had thought far enough ahead to envision himself actually arguing the case before a judge. Fin was also intrigued by Black's sharing that recommendation with them. But maybe he was just trying to scare them with the visual.

"Artist Richard Prince," Dyson continued, a little shakily, "has made a career of 'rephotographing' other works and publishing the pieces as his own, often with very little alteration. On April 25, 2013, it was ruled that Prince's use of the photographs was transformative and therefore was considered fair use. *Call of the Dragon* has been altered a lot more than Prince's photo art."

"Well, once again, Mr. Dyson, you're treadin' on dangerous ground when you talk about alterin' someone else's work." Black looked piercingly at Dyson, the amused smile still playing about his lips. "I'll admit I'm not familiar with this Richard Prince fella, or the court case concerning his work. But do you really feel confident enough to argue this before a judge?"

Dyson looked at Black, and at the other lawyers sitting beside him. Fin wondered if he saw himself as the underdog character in a Grisham novel, ultimately coming out on top when right wins against might, or if he was thinking about the legal powerhouse he would be going up against, not just Randall Black, but Universal Studios.

"'Cause I can tell ya right now that we're ready to take this to court," Black continued, gesturing toward his associates. "And besides the law and tons of legal precedents, we also have long years of experience on our side." That playful smile left his face now. "And I can guarantee ya that, once started, we will pursue damages to the fullest extent of the law."

As if carefully choreographed, one of his associates placed a folder on the table next to Black. Without looking at it, but keeping his eyes on Dyson, Black slid the folder in front of himself and opened it.

"Why don't we do a little ballparkin' to see how much that could cost ya, hmm?" He smiled at them again, and Fin felt his stomach drop in sympathy for the Intrepid people.

20

I'm not sure I want to go," Michelle said. She wished now that she hadn't used the last of her weed on the night of her fight with Mark. She was feeling hesitant, even scared, as she stood naked in front of her closet after a shower. She had always felt comfortable with her body, but more than that, she was hoping that displaying it now might put ideas into Mark's head, and influence him to want to make love to her and settle the issue, thus keeping her here for the evening.

She was encouraged when he looked up at her from the bed where he sat looking over some papers. She noticed him appreciating her curves, his eyes lingering at certain points.

"Why not?" he asked.

"I think I just feel like staying home." She didn't sound very convincing.

Mark looked at her askance. She sighed when she saw that he wasn't buying it, either. And he wasn't taking the bait.

"I don't know these people." She hated that she sounded like she was whining, but she couldn't help it.

"That's why you need to go, to get to know them." His tone was logical, as were the words, but she still felt apprehensive. "Honey, you've spent the last few months with just me. It's good that you've cut off ties with the friends who encouraged your old lifestyle, but I can't be everything for you. You need to make new friends."

"I know."

"That client who invited you, Amy?" Michelle nodded. "You said she's nice, and that she seems like someone you could be friends with." Michelle nodded again. "So, stick with her to begin with. You already, apparently, feel comfortable with her, or you wouldn't have accepted her invitation. So, you'll be there as her friend, and you can see what the others are like."

"I guess," Michelle sighed. "Can't you come, too?"

103

"Michelle, it's a girl's night out." His tone was edging toward annoyed, and Michelle knew she was being ridiculous. "Besides, I need to investigate this new venture. I have to get back to work." He sighed. "I felt safe paying off your house because of my investments. But the stock market's been plummeting lately, and I see I can't rely on that anymore. As they say, it takes money to make money, and I need to get started while I still have a little."

"I know I'm being childish," Michelle admitted. Mark laid the papers aside and stood up. Michelle turned hopefully toward him as he approached her.

"I know it might feel scary, starting this new life," he said, and Michelle thrilled, as she usually did, at the feel of his hands on her skin. "It might seem intimidating dipping your toe in a new pool. But it's something that needs to be done." He kissed her on her forehead, and she leaned against him as he wrapped his arms around her. "I just thought of something. My friend, Steve, is married. I'll give him a call. Maybe we can go out with him and his wife next week." Michelle sighed as she felt Mark's hands caress her bare back.

"But for now, you already have these plans. It's only for two or three hours. Get to know some new people, make a new friend or two, then you can come home." He moved his hand down around the curve of her naked buttock and pulled her up tight against him. "And here's a reminder that I'll be waiting here for you."

Michelle took in a deep, contented breath as she pressed her body against him, then groaned when he put his hands on her shoulders and pushed her away to look in her eyes. With a smartass grin on his face, he gave her a quick kiss on the lips, then winked.

"Have fun."

§

Michelle was happily surprised to find herself enjoying the evening.

The girls' night out was taking place at Tapa Vino, a new and highly rated dimly lit little wine bar in Lynn. It had been getting rave reviews, and Michelle could see why. The seating was comfortable, the music piped through the speakers, vaguely European, was quiet enough to hear but not too loud to have to shout to be heard. The walls were festooned with paintings and photographs of landscapes, scenery that could have been in parts of Mexico, Spain, Portugal, or even Italy or France.

Besides herself, there were four other women. First of all, there was Amy Johnson, her client, an accountant for a law firm, and she seemed to sense Michelle's angst and took her under her wing, introducing her to the others as they waited for a table.

The others were Judy Polanski, a very gregarious graphic designer who worked for an ad agency and was engaged to Amy's brother, Brian; Rachel Henry, who held some kind of administrative position at the State House in Boston; and Suzy Drummond whose parents had just died a month before. She had been living in Boston after college, and was trying to reconnect now with old friends, having recently moved back into her parents' house in Marblehead. She didn't say much at first, still kind of reeling from their loss, but she seemed nice.

The hostess told them their table was ready and led them to a round table near a fireplace.

"I feel like a Chardonnay," Amy announced as they settled around their table.

Looking at her slightly purplish black hair, Suzy said, "I'd say you look more like a Malbec."

She's quick, and a smartass, Michelle thought. She liked her but didn't really feel on the same level with her. In fact, she felt like all of them were a little above her, smarter, richer. The reminder of her origins just two weeks before, with the unfortunate visit with her mother, pounded into her head that she was just white trash in a nice dress.

"Chardonnay sounds good to me, too," Rachel said. Certain things, like warm smiles, fond looks, an occasional touch, told Michelle that Rachel and Suzy were good friends.

Everyone else agreed, and when the waiter arrived, a dark, handsome young man, they ordered a bottle and a charcuterie tray.

Michelle didn't feel comfortable saying anything about her addiction issues and was afraid that being the only one drinking something non-alcoholic might draw undue attention to it. So, she decided to have just one glass. After all, her main problem was with drugs, not alcohol.

"Your hair looks so cute," Judy said, looking at Amy's new cut.

"Thanks," Amy replied with a smile, turning her head both directions, apparently liking the feel of her dark, now shoulder-length hair. "Michelle did it. She's my new stylist and my hair's new best friend." She leaned toward Michelle, pressing their shoulders together.

Profuse praise ensued, followed by an in-depth discussion of each of their hair styles. Fortunately for Michelle, the women all had a good sense of style, so she was able to offer sincere compliments all around, with only minor suggestions of possible improvements.

"Looks like it's time for another bottle," Rachel said as she finished her glass of wine. Michelle looked at her glass and realized, to her surprise, that there was only a swallow left. She also realized that she wasn't feeling any ill effects.

After a brief discussion, they all agreed on the house Cabernet.

"So, Michelle," Judy said, "what do you like doing when you're not making other people beautiful?"

Michelle smiled and thought quickly. She didn't really have any hobbies. The expensive 'hobby' she used to have wasn't at all creative or constructive. She wished she was more like those who discussed what books they were reading at the moment, but her reading didn't really go far beyond **Vogue** or **Vanity Fair**. She racked her brain for other activities that might qualify.

"I like to cook," she said.

"Oh, yeah?" Rachel said. "What kind of things do you like to cook?"

"I love cooking with wine," Michelle replied. "Sometimes I even put it in the food." After that, she threw back that last swallow of wine from her glass, and then laughed, perhaps a little too loudly, she was afraid.

The others laughed, too, and Michelle felt a little more at ease. She enjoyed the feeling that suffused her body as she drank the wine. She had forgotten what it was like to feel outgoing and confident. It was nothing like the euphoria she used to get from the blow, but it helped. She had become somewhat withdrawn since Mark had helped her off the drugs, except when she got angry at him, like she did on Christmas Day. He could be so maddening sometimes.

In fact, when she was honest with herself, she could see how he seemed to feel somewhat possessive, if that was the right word. Almost dominating, as if he was her father. He had been so willing to put himself out there to help her off the drugs, and now, he seemed to think of himself as her savior.

Or maybe that was her own thinking.

But now, she felt almost like the life of the party again. She wasn't drunk, by any means, but she felt bold and fearless, and she loved the feeling.

She felt as if she was able to capture people's attention again, without feeling inferior or 'less than,' and her earlier thoughts of being white trash in a nice dress dissipated. These new friends seemed to accept her.

Then, there was Joaquin, the hot waiter who brought and opened the bottle of wine. She had noticed him watching her for a while, smiling when their eyes met, his gaze sweeping over her. Michelle knew she had a good body, and she didn't want it to go to waste. She liked having it appreciated.

And she found herself looking back.

She remembered Mark and feeling his hands on her naked body earlier. She squirmed a little in her chair as she thought about him, but then her thoughts shifted, and suddenly it was Joaquin who was holding her, and she felt an involuntary shiver, despite the warmth from the fireplace.

Joaquin didn't act as if he owned her. He didn't expect her honor and acclaim. He just wanted her. He just thought she was attractive.

As he poured wine into her glass, she looked at his hands, at the long, lean fingers gripping the bottle, imagining them holding her body. She glanced up at his face, and he returned the glance.

Without even thinking about it, she moved her arm slightly so that it just touched his thigh. He stayed there as he poured Amy's wine, pressing back a little, to let her know he noticed. Then, he moved around to the other side of the table to pour the other glasses.

"Is there anything else I can do for you?" he asked as he emptied the bottle, and he glanced at the other ladies before allowing his gaze to linger on Michelle. This time, he didn't smile. His face was decidedly more serious, more intense. The women glanced at each other, then looked at Joaquin and shook their heads.

By the time Michelle was halfway through her glass of Cabernet, her inhibitions had vanished. She was laughing at the others' jokes and throwing out quips of her own. And stealing meaningful glances at Joaquin. When he caught her eye, he glanced toward a hallway in the back, toward the restrooms. Her position at the table allowed her to look in that direction without turning around. When she looked back at him, she nodded almost imperceptibly.

The other women were talking about politics now, whether they thought Obama was doing a good job, or if they preferred McCain. Michelle didn't follow politics and found the subject boring in the extreme, though she had tried to at least look interested. She finished her Cabernet and glanced up at the waiter.

Joaquin said something to another waiter and pointed to his watch. The other waiter nodded, and Joaquin began walking back toward the hallway, with one last meaningful glance toward Michelle.

"Excuse me," Michelle said to Amy as she pushed her chair back. "I'll be back in a few minutes."

Amy nodded and turned back to the conversation.

Michelle walked a little unsteadily toward the hallway. Those two glasses of wine constituted the first alcohol she had had in several weeks, and it was hitting her a little harder than she had expected. Besides that, she didn't have experience with this sort of function. The other women were in jeans and blazers or sweaters. Michelle had dressed for a club, in a short dress and heels, and the heels had become a little unfamiliar in the last few months, as well.

The hallway was slightly dimmer than the main part of the wine bar, and she walked back to where she saw the restrooms. She walked past the ladies' room which opened off the hallway, toward the men's room which was in the corner where the hallway made a turn toward the right. She didn't see any sign of Joaquin, though.

"Psst," she heard from the right, and she saw a door open a crack. She cast a quick glance behind her, then turned the corner and went through the door, pulling it closed behind her. Joaquin reached around her and locked the door.

They were in a small supply room, lit by two flickering fluorescent tubes. One wall was lined with office supplies – waiter's order pads, pens, boxes of staples, a stack of old menus, and in the corner, a printer/fax machine. Another wall had a few miscellaneous kitchen items, and opposite that was a countertop, with boxes of printer paper underneath.

Joaquin touched Michelle's shoulder, and in an instant, she was in his arms, their lips and bodies squeezed together in a press of raw lust and passion. He tasted of wine and cigarettes. He picked her up under her arms and sat her on the countertop, still pressed against her as she wrapped her legs around him.

They parted long enough for him to lift her dress over her head, then they were back together, Joaquin fondling Michelle's breast as their tongues hungrily probed the other's mouths. When neither could take anymore, he dropped his pants while Michelle rocked back and forth a couple of times to pull her panties off. Joaquin produced a condom from his pocket, and it was in place in seconds.

Then, he was inside her, thrusting hard as she pulled her legs tighter against him, willing him deeper. His thrusts intensified until finally, he gasped and stopped, throbbing inside her, panting as he looked at her, his hunger now satisfied.

Michelle, not even breathing heavily from their rendezvous, remained there on the countertop for a few moments after he pulled out. She watched as Joaquin disposed of the condom in a trash can beside the printer/fax machine, and she idly wondered how many more were in there.

She sighed as she thought about Mark, and she knew she had fucked up big time, and to be honest, hadn't even gotten much out of it. Mark would have made sure that the sex was good for her as well.

Joaquin, on the other hand, hadn't spent any time satisfying her. The whole encounter lasted less than five minutes and they were dressed again. Michelle rejoined the ladies at the table, and a couple of them, she thought, looked a little strangely at her. The thought occurred to her that she probably should have stopped in the ladies' room to make sure her hair and makeup were still in order.

§

After her group of new friends broke up for the night, Michelle just drove around, trying not to panic. Should she tell Mark? Would there be any benefit in that?

There was little to no chance that he would ever find out. The other women didn't know what happened, and the wine bar was not a place that she and Mark would go to. Mark was more of a craft beer kind of guy.

Eventually, she found herself at Revere Beach, where she and Mark had gone for a walk at the end of their first date. She pulled over and parked by the bandstand and turned her car off. The lights along the walk were on, but their light was somewhat feeble. They illuminated the walk, but not much beyond it. There was no moon, and she couldn't see much of the beach, and nothing of the ocean, aside from the reflections of a few lights from Nahant across the sound.

Michelle got out of her car and stepped up onto the wide sidewalk, wandering aimlessly in and out of the soft overlapping circles of light that spread out along the walk. She let her thoughts travel back to that first night with Mark, and she remembered the anxiety she had felt, afraid that she might fuck up her chance with him. Given her record, she decided that that was always a good bet. She shook her head regretfully and sighed, trying to hold back the tears.

She didn't know how long she had been driving, or what time it was now, but there were few people about. So, she was surprised when she saw a man hunched over, apparently dozing in the dimmer area between the lights. His clothes were ragged and dirty, and without a further thought, Michelle snatched open her purse, digging around in it under the streetlamp. She found a twenty and a couple of singles, and she rushed over to him, her heels clacking loudly on the sidewalk.

He seemed startled by her sudden approach, and by her intense expression, but he relaxed when he saw the money in her outstretched hand.

"Thank you, ma'am," he said. He looked at the cash and saw the twenty, and he looked up at her. "Thank you!" he repeated more earnestly.

Michelle didn't trust her voice, so she just nodded. Then, with another sigh, she turned and started walking back toward her car, several blocks ahead of her now. Giving money to that homeless man, she reflected, didn't feel as good to her as it usually did. Before tonight, it always felt as if she was doing something altruistic, something that helped someone in need, and their expressed appreciation had always reinforced that feeling.

Now, she just felt as if she was trying to use a good deed to lessen the severity of what she did, to buy absolution for her sin. She had never been a religious person, but she wondered now if someone up there was keeping a tally, and if so, was there any valid way to atone for what she did?

She collapsed into her car and turned the key, but she didn't put the car in gear. She was on the verge of crying, and she didn't want to risk driving while her vision was blurry. She slipped her heels off and laid her head back against the headrest, closing her eyes in an attempt to hold back the tears.

Her earlier thoughts about being white trash returned as she remembered the brief, shallow sexual encounter with Joaquin. She had had many such encounters in the past, in clubs too numerous to recall. But she had not been in a relationship with the greatest guy in the world back then.

111

God, how could she be so stupid? Mark had demonstrated on so many occasions that he was kind and long-suffering. He gave up two weeks of his life to get her clean, for god's sake. He was so understanding. But she hadn't yet fucked up this badly. Could their relationship withstand something this huge?

She punched the knob on her radio with her knuckle and Apologize by OneRepublic was playing. She liked the song, and while she wasn't generally one to put much faith in mysticism or omens, she took it as a sign that she should tell Mark and apologize, beg for his forgiveness.

But as the song continued playing, the lyrics began seeping into her consciousness.

> I loved you with a fire red, now it's turning blue.
> And you say sorry like the angel heaven let me think was you.

She didn't know the limits of Mark's forgiveness, and she was afraid to test them.

> But I'm afraid it's too late to apologize.

As her tears pushed streaks of mascara down her cheeks, she knew she could never tell Mark about what happened tonight.

21

Suzy came out of the episode with tears streaming down her own cheeks. Her marriage to Mark had been, thankfully, free of any such missteps. She had been fastidiously faithful to Mark, never tempted to betray him. She had never even needed to consider asking his forgiveness for such an indiscretion.

But now, having just occupied Michelle's persona in this episode, Michelle's unfaithfulness felt like her own. And it was reinforced by her continued feeling of unfaithfulness to Fin.

She felt emotionally devastated.

"Michelle, why are you doing this to me?" she cried. Suzy felt Michelle's presence, and she smelled a sudden flair of sandalwood, but Michelle wouldn't show herself.

Suzy sat there, rooted in the chair, remembering the episode, and she recalled that evening. It was beyond strange, seeing herself there, and interacting with herself now from someone else's point of view. As if she were, somehow, disembodied, herself.

And she remembered that she had been one of the two who noticed Michelle's appearance when she returned to the table. Michelle just looked a little disheveled. Nothing that Suzy could really put her finger on for certain. She remembered noticing how beautiful and perfect she looked when she first met her. But when she came back from the restroom, her lipstick seemed just a bit smeared, her hair just a little mussed.

Now, she knew why.

§

"What's up with you lately?" Mark asked.

"What do you mean?" Michelle replied, her voice taut.

"I don't know, you just seem . . ." Mark shook his head, pondering, "especially attentive, almost clingy."

They were getting ready to go out with Mark's friend Steve, and his wife, Lou. Michelle was looking forward to making 'couple friends,' but she was also nervous.

"I just straightened your shirt, for fuck's sake," Michelle replied with a scoffing tone. But she knew what he meant. The guilt was eating her up.

During the past week, she always seemed to feel as if she had just taken a deep breath, but couldn't quite exhale it completely, her chest perpetually tight. Times like this, she felt the craving more than ever. Just a little bump would increase her confidence tenfold.

She was surprised to find that, without that chemical assistance, her guilt was leaving external indicators. She needed to be more careful.

It didn't help that the old needs had resurfaced with a vengeance. Not just the coke, but the sex. Mark was good, and he could always be counted on to satisfy her. When they did it. But two or three times a week just wasn't cutting it. He was always busy looking at his next business opportunity and Michelle found that she was manually satisfying herself multiple times a week.

The Fray's How to Save a Life started playing on the radio, and Michelle felt the tug she usually felt when she heard it. She sighed and turned her attention back to getting ready.

She had learned from the girls' night out, and from what Mark was wearing, and had toned down her outfit a little from what she had originally planned on wearing. She wore sprayed-on blue jeans, the kind that required her to jump two or three times to be able to tug them up over her butt to where she could fasten them. They were the only kind she owned.

She topped them off with a blue silk blouse that brought out the blue in her eyes, and a tweed blazer that was cut to hug her figure. A pair of heels, not quite as high as the ones she wore the week before, finished off her outfit.

"Damn!" Mark said, and Michelle turned to see him admiring her. "I feel like a slob next to you."

114

"Oh stop," she smiled, aware of the tingle that slithered down her body introduced by his look. "You look great." His jeans were considerably more casual than hers, his shirt, the one she had straightened, hung comfortably on him.

"Shit," he said, "I'm torn between wanting to take you out and show you off or wishing I could rip those clothes off your body and make love to you." Michelle felt a familiar warmth between her legs, and she sighed and wished for the second option. God, she needed a good fuck!

Looking her over a bit more, Mark turned and pulled a blazer out of the closet and dressed up his look just a bit.

She smiled and leaned forward to kiss him, her hands on his waist, but she made it a point to let go before she seemed clingy. They left a few minutes later.

As they drove, the route they took seemed familiar to Michelle. "Where are we going?" she asked.

"It's called Tapa Vino. It's some new wine bar in Lynn that Lou's been wanting to try."

Michelle suddenly felt a lead weight in her stomach. Of all the stupid coincidences, this was definitely the worst that she could imagine.

"But you don't like wine," she said, her voice quiet in an attempt to keep it steady.

"Oh, it's okay," he hedged. "It's not my favorite, but I'm sure they'll have beer there, too. I guess the place has gotten really good ratings. Steve said Lou's been badgering him to try it since the place opened."

Mark glanced over at Michelle. The expression on his face as he looked at her made her afraid that he could see what she was thinking.

"You said alcohol doesn't have as big a pull on you as cocaine and other drugs," he said with a concerned voice, "so I didn't think it would be a problem. Was I wrong?"

Michelle felt a momentary relief that she had been mistaken about his mind-reading ability, but the fact remained that they were returning to the scene of her crime. She shook her head in response to Mark's question.

"You can have water or tea if you prefer," Mark continued helpfully. "Or, if you do want to have a glass of wine, if you want me to, I can discreetly monitor how much you drink. But only if you want me to."

Michelle looked away, her eyes misting at the concern he was expressing, in contrast to how little she deserved it.

"No, you don't have to do that," she said. "I'll be fine. But thank you."

When they entered the restaurant, Michelle's eyes quickly took in the whole place, rapidly darting around in all directions. To her immense relief, she didn't see Joaquin. Steve and Lou were already seated, and Mark took Michelle's hand and led her to the table.

Michelle liked Steve and Lou, but she experienced the same feelings of inferiority that she had initially felt with the ladies the week before. They were both well-educated and shared Mark's sharp sense of humor, and they seemed to closely follow current events. Michelle felt as if she couldn't keep up with them. She hoped a glass of wine would help to ease her inhibitions, as it had the week before.

When Joaquin appeared at their table, her heart dropped. She felt his hands on her again, felt him inside her. He, quite obviously, recognized her, and he looked curiously at Mark. Michelle couldn't tell if Joaquin's face indicated fear of exposure, or a feeling of longing.

She managed to put in her order for a glass of Pinot noir, and she hoped it came quickly.

§

"Well," Mark said, in response to the question, "I really liked The Bourne Ultimatum, but I don't know that I liked it better than the original movie, or the sequel." He thought a moment longer, then shook his head. "I don't think I can pick a single movie. I'm going to say my favorite movie is the Bourne trilogy."

"What a cop out," Steve chided good naturedly.

They were playing a game that, apparently, had grown out of an old seventies movie, The Way We Were, which had been a favorite of one of Steve's early girlfriends. In the movie, Robert

Redford's character, Hubbell, and his best friend, J.J., engaged in a game in which one would prompt 'Best Saturday afternoon,' or 'Best month,' or 'Best year,' after which the other would answer. Lou's prompt had been "Best movie." In their version, they went around the table, and each gave an answer.

Michelle had almost said that **Shrek** was her favorite but, remembering a movie she had seen a few months ago with Mark, she instead had named **The Ultimate Gift**. The others nodded in appreciation of the movie, and she felt that she might have risen a bit in their eyes.

It was purely a matter of opinion, of course, but Michelle had found it interesting. When she could focus on it, at least. Joaquin was, to say the least, a distraction. By this time Michelle was on her second glass of wine, and it wasn't doing much to ease the tension that had settled in her gut.

It seemed that, every time she had purged the memory of her indiscretion with him from her mind, he appeared at their table to see if they needed anything. When she ordered another glass of Pinot, her third, she sensed Mark's look, but she didn't direct her attention to him.

When she was a teen, her brother, Nicky, had tried learning to play the guitar a bit. He was never any good, but Michelle remembered when he would tune it, especially after changing the strings, how she cringed when he kept tightening the high E string. The higher the tone, she just knew the string was going to snap.

Her body felt as tight as that guitar string. Every time Joaquin showed up, it felt like Nicky turning the key, stretching that wire almost to its breaking point, sharp tones sounding every time the string suddenly stretched a bit. When Joaquin placed her latest order in front of her, she picked it up without looking at him, and took another drink. She sighed, but still didn't feel any better.

"Okay," Steve said, "let's make it a little more interesting." He grinned diabolically. "Stupidest thing you've ever done." Groans were uttered and eyes were rolled. "Lou," Steve continued, "you start."

Lou sighed and looked around. She seemed a little embarrassed, but it was a lighthearted game, and she smiled a little nervously. She leaned forward and lowered her voice.

"Alright, here goes." The rest of them leaned forward, as well, in subconscious anticipation.

"In college," she began, "my roommate and I spent a semester seeing if we were in love with each other."

"Wait," Mark said, "your roommate Olivia?" Michelle couldn't remember if Mark knew Lou in college, or if he just remembered Olivia was her roommate from other stories. Lou nodded regretfully. "What do you mean by 'seeing if you were in love'?" Mark asked, his eyelids narrowed.

"It started out with kissing," Lou replied, "you know, just to see what it felt like. Neither one of us had a boyfriend at the time, so we figured what the hell. From there, it progressed to some pretty heavy making out, and finally to sleeping together a couple of times."

"Okay," Steve grinned, his voice drenched with intrigue, "I'm going to need to revisit this in a little more detail later on in private."

"No, you won't," Lou said, her voice firm and decisive. When Steve hesitated to respond appropriately, Lou raised an eyebrow, her piercing gaze never leaving his face, and Steve reluctantly backed down.

"Okay, fine. Still, why do you say this was the stupidest thing you've ever done?"

"Because we weren't gay."

"Well, obviously. But still I can see this being attributed to just normal experimentation."

"That's true. So, maybe that wasn't the stupidest thing." Lou looked sheepishly at the rest of them. "But leaving the door unlocked is probably a contender. After Margie McGee walked in on us, it didn't take long for it to get all over campus. Neither one of us could get a boyfriend for the rest of the year."

"What were the two of you doing when she walked in on you?" Steve asked, his face a little too eager.

"Steve," Lou said in a warning voice.

"Okay, fine." Steve sat back with his arms folded, looking like a scolded child.

Mark, still smiling from their exchange, looked at Steve.

"What about you, Steve? What was the stupidest thing you ever did?"

"Agreeing to not pursue the details of Lou's lesbian lore." Mark and Lou both snickered at him.

During all of that, Michelle had been flipping through the mental Rolodex of stupid things she had done, and she had to admit the list was considerable. Most of them involved either drugs, sex or alcohol, or a seemingly endless combination. It was just a matter of picking one.

She remembered the feeling of confidence that would flood her body and mind when she snorted a little coke. Times of stress, like right now, she really felt that craving.

Being so focused on picking something to say for her turn, she only gave partial attention to Lou and Steve's dialogue. Thus, Steve noticed that she hadn't snickered when Mark and Lou did. As she was taking another drink of wine, she jumped when Steve addressed her.

"Michelle?" He smiled and gestured toward her as if inviting her to contribute. "Stupidest thing you've ever done."

She put her glass down and sighed, wiping her lip, the alcohol swirling around in her brain. As she saw Joaquin across the room, she knew there was one thing she absolutely could not say, so she just needed to pick one of the others.

"I left my friends at that table over there to fuck that waiter in a storage room."

It took a couple of seconds for it to register that she had actually named the one thing she had resolved that she wouldn't say. It was the silence and the shocked expressions on the faces of the others that finally hammered it through the alcoholic fog and into her consciousness.

"Excuse me?" Mark said quietly. Michelle looked at him and could see the anger stewing under the surface as he turned to look squarely into her eyes. She slapped her hands over her face as she felt it flush. "This was just last week?"

She looked up at him again, and she saw Steve and Lou exchange an uncomfortable glance. She nodded her head, feeling as if all the air had been ripped from her lungs.

"You're always so busy looking at those fucking papers," she finally managed to say.

Mark continued to look at her, his face inscrutable as a slab of stone, a vein throbbing in his temple. Finally, he inhaled as he turned.

"Steve, Lou," he said almost in a whisper, his voice unnaturally, ominously calm, as he counted out a few twenties from his wallet, "I'm sorry, but I think it might be best if we leave now." They both nodded, silent, looking uncomfortably at Mark and Michelle.

As they stood up, Joaquin approached the table, but he stopped when he saw the expression on Mark's face, and Michelle's.

Michelle followed Mark outside, holding her breath.

He stopped when he reached his car and just stood there, silently staring straight ahead, but Michelle could hear the breath rushing in and out through his nostrils, see the clouds of steam that puffed with each exhalation. Finally, he turned toward her, his face peculiarly shadowed by the lights and the bare trees in the parking lot.

"So, let me get this straight," he said, his voice still quiet and nearly toneless. "You came here last week and fucked the waiter, then went home and crawled into bed with me?"

"Mark, it was stupid, I know," Michelle replied.

"Oh, you think?" His voice took on a little more life as his anger began to claw through his reserve. "And then to blame it on me?" Michelle frowned at him, and Mark realized he needed to remind her. "'I'm always so busy looking at those papers.' Yeah, after I took two weeks off to get you clean, and after I paid off your house, I kind of need to get back to work."

"It's not just that," Michelle resisted, "but you teased me then, too."

"What?" Mark asked, his face screwed up in confusion.

"Before I came here last week, when I was naked, you came and held me and kissed me, and you got me all hot. Then you pushed me away."

Mark's eyes were wide by the time she finished, and Michelle knew why. That excuse sounded weak to her, too.

"So you talk to me about it," Mark replied, his voice rising. "You don't just go out and fuck the first guy you see!"

Just then, a couple walked out of the restaurant, and Mark, frustrated, quieted down and pointed to the car.

"Get in," he said, his voice suddenly toneless and dispassionate. "We need to get home." Michelle slid in as Mark slammed his door. "I'll sleep on the couch in my office tonight. I'll find another place tomorrow."

Michelle felt a sudden stab of fear, realizing that she was losing Mark, if she hadn't already. She couldn't let him go.

"Mark, please, let's work this out."

"Work it out? How do you suggest we work this out?"

"I made a stupid mistake," Michelle pleaded. "But it was just sex. It didn't mean anything to me."

Mark scoffed.

"Well, I have to say that it kind of means something to me."

"I love you!" Michelle insisted.

"Yeah? I can't help but think that fucking another man in a supply closet is a really odd way to express how much you love me."

"Mark," she said, sobbing now, "I couldn't help it. It was just part of my stupid fucking addictions." God, never in her life had she needed a snort as badly as she did now.

Mark turned and looked at her.

"Addictions?"

"I used to go home with somebody different almost every night. Now, we have sex two, maybe three times a week, and it's just not enough."

Mark sat there, still looking at her, his eyebrows pulled together, thinking about what she had said.

"Are you telling me you're a sex addict, too?"

Michelle looked at him and pondered her response. Which would give the best result?

"I don't know," she replied while wiping the tears away, hoping that ambiguity might be the best option.

"Shit," Mark whispered as he turned and looked out the windshield toward the street. Michelle watched quietly, willing him to take pity on her. After a few seconds, he shook his head. "I don't think I can do this," he uttered under his breath.

"Please, Mark," Michelle begged, "I don't want to lose you. It'll never happen again, I swear!"

A painfully long time passed before Mark spoke again, and even then, it seemed to be an effort for him get it out. Michelle struggled to see the love through the disgust in his eyes.

"If this goes on any longer," he said quietly, his voice straining for control, "and I don't know if it can, but IF it does, there need to be some major adjustments."

"I understand, Mark," Michelle replied enthusiastically. "Anything. I'll do anything."

"First and foremost is that you need to get some counseling. Obviously, there's more involved than just getting you off the shit, and I clearly don't have the necessary knowledge or skill set. And start going to AA, or whatever they have for drug addicts and sex addicts."

"Okay," Michelle said, a little less enthusiastically. The idea scared her, but not as much as losing Mark.

"God, I was an idiot to think that I could fix you all by myself."

"Well, that's what guys do, right?" Michelle said with an attempted smile.

Mark looked at her, apparently not appreciating the humor quite as much as she did.

"I'll still be sleeping on the couch tonight," he said. "I'm still pretty disgusted by this whole shitshow."

He reached up and turned the key and he started driving toward home.

22

Fin sat back in his chair, rocking a little, and nervously rotating it back and forth. Overall, there was a light-hearted air in the conference room. The people from Intrepid Studios had excused themselves, after being directed to another room where they could consult together. The dollar amounts that Randall Black had quoted, based on other infringement cases they had prosecuted, seemed to take the wind out of their sails.

The Universal lawyers were joking around with each other, clearly confident in the outcome of this meeting. Daryl, Fin's agent, had moved to the end of the room, near the windows and away from the others, to listen to messages and return phone calls. Fin's stomach was in an upheaval as they waited.

Finally, after nearly a half hour, the three from Intrepid filed back into the conference room. They sat down in the chairs they had previously occupied, while everyone else looked expectantly at them.

Dyson took a deep breath and, after a nervous glance at his companions, looked at Randall Black.

"Mr. Black, it has been decided that it is in Intrepid Studios' best interests to continue with the production of *Call of the Dragon*. We feel that the screenplay is, at best, an original work, and at worst, a transformative one, and are confident in the authenticity and originality of the work."

Dyson seemed to struggle to swallow before he continued. "Furthermore, since Universal does not even have a contract with Mr. Jones to produce an adaptation of his novel, *DragonCache*, we feel that you are out of line, and that it is inappropriate for Universal to be litigating any charges against Intrepid Studios."

John Whitson looked smugly at those across the table from him. Jeremy Dyson and Marion Plum didn't seem nearly as confident.

What they lacked in confidence, though, Randall Black made up for. He smiled, and Fin had a sudden impression of a lion surveying a herd of lame antelope. He almost expected Black to lick his lips.

"Well, Mr. Dyson," Black said, "and Mr. Whitson and Ms. Plum, I'm really sorry to hear you say that. As we have negotiated with Mr. Jones in the past for previous movie adaptations, we are confident in the outcome of this particular case, and we'll be happy to meet you in court where we will proceed to throw the fuckin' book at y'all."

"Bring it on, asshole," Whitson blustered, while Dyson cringed, placing a restraining hand on his arm.

Black's smile was even bigger now as he and his team began gathering up the folders and papers that had been used during the meeting. The one Universal executive who was sitting in on the meeting put his pen in his pocket, along with the little notebook he had scratched some notes on. Even though he had nothing to gather up, he waited for the lawyers.

Fin watched the wrap-up of the meeting with some chagrin. This was not the way he had hoped it would turn out. Daryl looked at him, raised his eyebrows and shrugged. He started to push his chair back but stopped when Fin leaned forward.

"Hold on," Fin said. Everyone looked at him, surprise showing on most of the faces. None of them were more surprised than he was. "I'm not happy with the way this is being left."

"Well, Mr. Jones," Black replied, "that's what the courtroom is for."

"No, this doesn't need to go to court."

"I'm sorry, son," Black wore a confused look now, "don't you agree with what we said here?"

"In general, yes," Fin replied. He looked at Randall Black. "The fact is, Mr. Black, you *are* a bit of an asshole." Whitson snickered, and Fin turned to him. "Mr. Whitson, I think you are, too."

The air suddenly felt a little more charged, and Fin wondered what he had gotten himself into.

23

Golden rays of light slanted through the front window from the setting sun. The light cast a crisscrossing design from the muntins of the window, warping the pattern across the curves of Suzy's body in the wing-back chair. As the sun sank lower, the heat gradually drained from its light, and Suzy felt a shiver.

She had spent a half hour driving home to feed Ursula, then another half hour driving back to Saugus. Ursula had happily bounced around when Suzy first showed up, ecstatic to see her second favorite human, but the disappointment quickly descended over her as Suzy left again.

Now, feeling emotionally drained, Suzy struggled to regain the level of relaxation she needed to be able to enter the next episode. She closed her eyes and concentrated on breathing deeply and slowly. But it was hard. Her body was a bundle of nerves, her heart racing as if she was the one who was in danger of losing Mark.

Finally, she began to feel the familiar swirly sensation in her head, at the exact same time that she experienced that prickly impression of someone watching her.

She opened her eyes and looked around, just as Michelle's world settled in around her.

§

Michelle looked in the rear-view mirror, brushing the powder from her nose, and she turned the key to start her drive home. Terry, the homeless man on the corner, had been very appreciative of the singles she had handed him. She smiled at the memory, but she felt a similar feeling to what she had experienced on the fateful night with Joaquin. Did giving money to homeless people count as a selfless, altruistic act, or was she merely trying to atone for her sins?

She sighed as she merged with traffic on Tobin Memorial, remembering that night, and every night since then. Mark hadn't moved out, but ever since that night, he had been sleeping on the lumpy couch in the office. They didn't talk much, and Michelle didn't know what kind of hours he had been keeping. It had been almost two months now, and they had simply settled into a dreary routine.

He had decided on a new venture, though Michelle didn't really know much about it. She had asked, hoping that he would appreciate her interest, but his description had been pretty scientific and had largely gone over her head. She knew it had to do with some kind of technology to draw moisture out of the air in places that didn't have enough clean drinking water, but beyond that, she was in the dark.

When he wasn't working on that, he spent time out of the house, presumably pursuing gadgets and information related to that project. Then, he would spend the night on the sofa.

When Michelle saw him, at dinner time, mainly, his face was drawn, his eyes lethargic, even sad, she thought. Definitely disconnected from Michelle. In the past, when she got home from work, she would often change into loose, comfy sweats. The last few weeks, she had made it a point to either keep on what she had worn to work or change into something more revealing. She desperately needed to get Mark back.

So far, there had been no change with him.

She had begun attending meetings of Cocaine Anonymous. The meetings were after work in Andover, a thirty-minute drive from work and from home, so that kept her away a whole day every week.

After about a week of Mark's disapproval and sleeping in the office, even after she had started attending the meetings, she had confronted him about it.

"When are you going to join me in our bed?" she had asked, placing a little extra emphasis on the word 'our,'

Mark had looked at her a few seconds before responding.

"I'm not sure if I will or not."

Michelle scoffed.

"But you said you wanted me to join those twelve-step programs," she had replied hotly. "I've done that."

"I said that needed to happen, but I also made it clear that it would not be a guarantee." He had narrowed his eyes at her. "I don't know, yet, if we can get past this. But it's going to take a lot more than one week to determine if there will be any change and if we have any chance of survival."

She had started to respond angrily to him, but at the time, she was clear-headed enough to know that it would only push him further away. So, she had backed off.

But it was driving her crazy.

The following week, she made a call to Candy, the dealer who used to keep her supplied. He was disappointed that she only wanted a small amount, but was happy to hear from her, nevertheless.

She only purchased two 8 balls from him. Those wouldn't have lasted her very long in the past, but she had a plan. She knew she had been overdoing it before. She had been off the stuff for about a month by this time, so she just wanted a small amount for maintenance, just to manage the craving when it appeared.

So far, Mark hadn't given any indication that he noticed any difference in her behavior after she had snorted a small bump from her fingernail. She didn't use it every day, just when she needed a little boost. It barely did anything for her, just took the edge off, so it didn't make her crazy like the Sunday when Mark had discovered her problem.

It seemed she needed it most when Mark was around, exuding his disapproval of her.

She had also joined a Sexaholics Anonymous group in Cambridge, at Mark's urging.

The meetings, in both cases, were grueling, listening to the others going on about the problems they were having staying off the drugs and off sex. With the Sexaholics Anonymous group, the unmarried people were supposed to stay off sex completely, including masturbation. Michelle, since she still considered herself in a relationship with Mark, didn't think of herself as single so, taking advantage of a technicality, she didn't take it that far. Granted, they hadn't had sex in a couple of months, but she still satisfied herself whenever the need arose.

When she thought about it, she knew that, in both cases, she was certainly undermining the twelve-step programs, defeating their purpose. So, she tried to make it a point to not think about it.

Still, she was quite dissatisfied with the time she had with Mark.

She didn't know how he felt about their time together.

§

"Mark, please don't make me go to this alone," Michelle pleaded as they sat at the dinner table.

"I don't even know these people," Mark countered, his voice a monotone.

"I know, but they're my friends. I've been talking you up to them."

"Seems kind of silly since we're nothing but roommates."

"You know that's not what I want, though," Michelle said.

"I know," Mark replied quietly.

Michelle's new friend, Judy Polanski, the graphic designer who was marrying Amy's brother, had invited her to her wedding. Michelle didn't really know why, but in hopes that she could ingratiate herself with her new friend, Michelle had accepted the invitation. The wedding was in two days.

Mark, taking an inordinately long time between bites, finally looked up at Michelle.

"Okay, fine, I'll go with you to the wedding."

"Thank you, sweetheart," Michelle replied, her eyes tearing up as they often did recently. She put her hand to her head as she felt the ache, but she smiled at Mark.

"What's the matter?" he asked.

"Oh, nothing," she replied, moving her hand. Over the last few weeks, the headache had been appearing nearly every evening, along with the fatigue, but she didn't want to distract Mark. She desperately hoped that he would eventually forgive her stupidity and come back to her.

God, she needed to feel him next to her, and inside her. Especially inside her. But that was more than just a physical need. She knew it was an emotional one and, from the Sexaholics Anonymous meetings, a psychological one.

But it was a need she desperately needed to satisfy.

§

The first Saturday of spring was a little chilly, but the wedding had been lovely. Michelle had never spent much time in churches, but the imposing two-hundred-year-old Gothic-Romanesque-style Episcopal Church in Lynn was a beautiful setting for Judy and Brian's simple wedding. The reception was held in a historic inn near Revere Beach.

As Michelle and Mark entered the reception hall, they hung up their jackets and looked around as an 80s cover band cranked out Eye of the Tiger. *A few people were on the small dance floor that had been cleared in front of the stage, bouncing and gyrating to the throbbing beat.*

Michelle was looking around for her friends. Mark, she assumed, was looking for the food and drinks, as he had not had any lunch.

Having divested herself of her jacket, Michelle slipped her hand through the crook of Mark's arm, squeezing it affectionately. It had been a long time since he had permitted her this much closeness and contact. She hoped it wasn't just to keep from embarrassing her in front of her friends, but that it was a precursor to allowing her back in his life and getting him back into her bed. But knowing Mark and his thoughtfulness, even now, Michelle knew that the first option was a definite contender.

Despite the cool temperature, she was wearing a short, flimsy dress with a sexy sheer lace insert that meandered sinuously from the high collar, down between her breasts and ended at the waistline. It clung to her body in all the right places, leaving only a little to the imagination.

Michelle knew it was kind of slutty, but she was feeling desperate. In all her adult life, she had never gone two months without sex. That memory of Nicky tuning his guitar had been on her mind a lot lately. Her body felt as tight as that high E string, on the verge of snapping. She felt that need even more strongly than she needed a snort. Masturbating was good, but it wasn't the same. The physical release was there, but it did nothing for her intense emotional need.

She had caught Mark looking at her a number of times, which reinforced her thought that his feelings might be softening toward her.

She had noticed a number of other guys looking at her, too. She was definitely cool with that. Not only was it good for her self-esteem, but she figured that if she noticed it, Mark likely did, too. A little healthy dose of jealousy could certainly help her situation right now.

As she looked around, she saw Judy and Brian, and she pulled Mark toward them. He was gracious, greeting them warmly and congratulating them. While he chatted with Brian, Michelle hugged Judy.

"Damn, girl," Judy said, looking her up and down, "don't you know you're not supposed to go to a wedding looking better than the bride?"

"Oh, you're so sweet," Michelle said, feeling her face flush a little. "But you're wrong. You're the most beautiful thing here."

"Aw, thank you," Judy replied, putting a finger up to the corner of her eye as if to wipe away a tear. "And thank you for coming."

"I'm so glad you invited me. I haven't been to a wedding in a long time." Michelle looked around. "Although I'm afraid I don't know anybody."

"Sure you do," Judy said. "You know me." Michelle nodded and smiled. "And there's Amy over there. And you haven't met him yet, but that's her fiancé, Jason." Judy scanned the room a bit more. "Oh, and there's Suzy." Judy pointed to her maid of honor, swathed in her lavender bridesmaid dress, busily organizing the gift table.

Michelle glanced back at Mark and smiled at him, and as he listened to Brian, he looked at her, his face a blank. There was no warmth showing on it. Maybe he was just focused on whatever Brian was talking about, but she couldn't help but wonder if she might have misread that closeness and contact that he had allowed earlier.

As she continued engaging in small talk with Judy, that thought kept chewing at the back of her brain. She felt as if she was no closer to getting him back now than she had been two months ago.

Somebody else approached and wanted to greet the bride, so Michelle excused herself. When she turned toward Mark, he wasn't there. Someone else was talking to Brian.

Michelle scanned the room again, looking for Mark, trying not to let the growing panic take hold. She saw him looking over the finger foods spread out on a table at the other end of the hall. She nearly sobbed when she saw that he hadn't left her.

At the same time, though, she was growing more certain that he actually had.

§

Ever since they had arrived, Michelle's agitation had not eased at all. She had gone looking for the restrooms, her desperation growing, but she didn't find them. In the process, though, she stumbled into a storage room, and knew that it would suffice for satisfying her current pressing need.

She frantically dug into her purse as the band finished Don't Stop Believin', muffled now through the walls. She found the tiny plastic bag, squeezing the little clip that she used to keep it closed. Untwisting the top, she dipped her pinky fingernail into the powder inside and, pressing her thumb against her right nostril, sniffed it up her left nostril. It helped, but she was feeling particularly anxious now. She dipped it again and sniffed it up the right nostril and heaved a sigh of relief, as I Melt With You started on the other side of the wall.

Her anxiety was gradually replaced, now, by confidence. The doubts that assailed her earlier were gone, or at least, not as intense. She felt good about herself. It wasn't the wave of euphoria that she used to experience when she would do a couple of lines, but it definitely helped. She felt a little more balanced, a little more convinced of her own value, even if Mark wasn't.

Fuckin' Mark! she thought, but felt guilty immediately.

132

She twisted the bag closed and replaced the clip, dropping what was left of the 8 ball back into her purse. She stood up straight and took a deep breath, carefully wiping her nostrils, and turning quickly as the door opened.

She recognized the man standing there. Or rather, she recognized the deep plum-colored tuxedo he was wearing. It was Doug, Brian's best man.

"Oh, hi," he said. The extremely casual way he said it, countered by the intensity of his expression, made it difficult for Michelle to determine if the encounter was accidental or not. "Are you okay?" he asked when she didn't respond.

"I am now," Michelle replied. Feeling the bump doing its job, she felt more than okay. But she realized, from the carnal grin that appeared on Doug's face, that he assumed she meant that she was okay now because he was there.

He closed the door behind him and let his eyes do a slow, exploratory tour of her body. They lingered on her legs and on the fine lace panel that showed the inner curves of her breasts.

The sheer lust that showed on his face was enough to start that wet tingle between her legs. It was the look that she loved and missed getting from Mark. But even from this stranger, it was enough to accelerate her breathing.

She felt the old flush as her brain released dopamine and other chemicals into her bloodstream, supplementing the beginning rush of the cocaine, nudging her a little closer to that old feeling of euphoria.

Michelle dropped her purse and turned to fully face Doug. As he approached her, she really hoped that she had been wrong about Mark's feelings about her. She missed his warmth, his thoughtfulness, his touch. She really needed to get him back.

But as Doug reached her and touched her, sending a shiver through her body, she knew the accuracy of her interpretation of Mark's feelings didn't matter.

There was no way he would ever take her back after this.

§

There were a number of vinyl-covered pads stacked up in the corner, like gymnastic mats, and that's where Michelle and

Doug ended up. It was certainly more comfortable than the countertop in the restaurant.

And Doug was a little more attentive than Joaquin. Not as much as Mark, of course. Michelle couldn't stop herself from comparing. But Doug was a little more concerned with her satisfaction than Joaquin had been.

It had been so long that just the feel of him thrusting in and out of her was almost enough to make her cum, as Another One Bites the Dust *pounded in the main part of the hall. But Doug also did a little clitoral manipulation, obviously hoping she enjoyed it, as well.*

After he climaxed, as he lay on top of her, looking into her eyes, he kissed her, and Michelle felt a tug at her heart. He didn't just pull out, get dressed and leave. He was tender, and it brought a tear to her eye.

As Livin' On a Prayer *started, the music suddenly became louder and clearer, and Michelle heard voices nearby.*

"I saw some more chairs over there in the corner," said a man, and Michelle's heart jumped as she realized that the door had been opened. "We can help you with them."

"Oh, thank you so much," a woman responded.

Doug quickly reached around him and found his tuxedo, whipping the coat over on top of them, pulling out of Michelle in the process.

"Jesus Christ!" the woman shrieked, clearly startled to find them there. "Doug," she said, her shock turning to embarrassment, "I didn't know you and Monica were in here."

Michelle turned toward the voice and saw a woman she recognized from the church, the groom's mother. The shock on her face suddenly intensified, her hand on her chest to try to calm her breathing.

"You're not Monica."

"Mrs. McKay, I —" Doug fumbled for words, and Michelle felt his penis dangling between her legs, abruptly flaccid, swinging and bumping against her like the clapper on a bell.

Mrs. McKay immediately turned away. There were three people, dressed up for the wedding, accompanying her. Two of them

134

felt no such compunction, and Michelle thought she saw the shadow of a grin on one of their faces.

"I-I-I'll be out in a minute," Doug stuttered. Mrs. McKay rushed out of the room, reluctantly followed by the others.

§

Mark was sitting at a table with Suzy, apparently deeply involved in conversation, when Michelle emerged from the storage room. Doug had left a couple of minutes before, with barely a look at Michelle.

She stood there in the doorway for a moment, contemplating what to do, as the band started playing With Or Without You. She didn't know if word had gotten around yet. She took a deep, quivering breath, and decided, hopefully, to try a direct approach.

"Mark," she said as she got to the table, "I'm ready to go whenever you are." Knowing that he hadn't wanted to come in the first place, she figured he'd jump at the chance to leave.

Instead, he looked at her coldly, his face frostier than she had ever seen it, then turned back to Suzy. And Michelle realized that he knew.

Suddenly, Michelle could feel every eye in the place boring into her. The little bit of cocaine in her system was, by now, just enough to heighten her awareness, but not enough for her to not give a fuck.

She looked around the hall, seeing the looks of disgust from so many people, most of whom she didn't even know. If looks could kill, as the saying went.

At this moment, she wished they could.

> I can't live
> with or without you.

There was no way around it now. She had lost Mark. And she had done it in the most embarrassing way possible. Feeling the tears springing to her eyes, feeling her face flush hot, she turned and fled the hall, grabbing her jacket on the way out, as the band taunted her.

And you give yourself away.
And you give yourself away.

As she ran away from the hall, she turned her ankle, skidding
on the asphalt, skinning her knees and her palms. She stopped
and sat on the hood of a car to take her heels off, knuckling the
incessant tears from her eyes.

Reaching into her purse, she fished out her cell phone and, be-
tween sobs, called a cab, then limped barefoot on the cold side-
walk toward North Shore Road to wait for it.

§

Suzy came out of the episode with tears streaming
down her cheeks. First, the tears were there because of the
residual emotion from Michelle for having lost Mark. After
she was out of the episode, though, Michelle's emotions
were replaced with her own as she replayed her initial
meeting with Mark that day all those years ago.

She allowed herself to cry for a minute or two, then she
forced herself to take a deep breath.

"God dammit, Suzy," she said aloud, "get your shit together. He's been dead for years now."

The words sounded harsh to her own ears, and while
she could easily accept the logic of the statement, the emotion was still strong after spending this surrogate time
with him.

Still, she knew she needed to get through the episodes
and be able to help Michelle to move on. But she could still
not imagine why Michelle was showing her this.

There were slight anomalies in her own memory of that
day. For instance, she remembered Mark telling her that
Michelle was a friend of Brian's and not Judy's. She remembered sitting on the other side of Mark at the table
when Michelle came to them. Minor differences, but it was
enough to make her wonder how accurate these episodes
really were, if they were based on potentially faulty memories.

136

Suddenly, she remembered the feeling she had experienced just before entering the episode, the sensation of being watched. She turned and looked out the window. It was dark outside now, but there were no lights on in the house, either, so she could see outside easily enough. The streetlight across the street illuminated the road for a few houses in each direction, but Suzy couldn't see anyone.

But the memory was enough to make her shiver.

24

He couldn't figure out what was going on. The older woman was gone, but now, this younger woman was there, and she seemed to have taken up residence in that chair in the living room. Sitting in his car, across the street and two houses down, he could just make her out through the window as the lowering sun shone through the living room window.

He wore a T-shirt and shorts, and he had every window in his old grey Honda rolled down, but the July sun beating down on the car had been baking him. He grasped the neck of the shirt and flapped it several times, allowing the air to cool the perspiration that soaked it, temporarily cooling him. But it was only a momentary measure, one that had been repeated numerous times before, and likely would be again.

He knew he had almost been caught earlier. He had been following a little too closely. She had started driving somewhat erratically, speeding up a little, then slowing down, as if trying to decide what to do.

When she quickly veered off onto Summer Street instead of signaling and calmly making the turn like all the others, he knew for certain that she had seen him. By this time, he knew where she was going. He didn't need to actually follow her the rest of the way. He continued past on Neptune when she turned.

Several hours later, when she left again, he knew to stay farther back and to not duplicate her moves immediately. It was harder to keep her in sight, but with practice, he managed.

That time, she went to a house on Marblehead Neck, a large, castle-like structure, and was there for only about a half hour. After that, she returned and, once again, installed herself in the chair by the living room window.

He just couldn't figure it out.

Suddenly, she jerked and turned toward the window, looking around as if she knew that someone was out there. Instinctively, he slouched down behind the dashboard, but just as quickly, she seemed to relax, and her head settled down onto her shoulder.

He just couldn't figure out what was going on.

He sighed as he looked at his watch. It was going to be a long night. He hadn't gotten much sleep, and he really needed to go now.

He started up his Honda and drove away.

25

Fin sat at a table in the hotel restaurant, scarfing down his dinner, thinking about what had happened. He had thought about searching out some famous restaurant, perhaps one frequented by the stars, but he decided that, after the adrenaline had cleared out of his system, he was just a little too wiped out to bother.

But he was starving.

Earlier that afternoon, in the Universal Studios conference room, he had been on a roll. After he had called the two top-ranking men in the room assholes, he continued.

"I think we can do better than taking this to court," he said.

"Well, son," Randall Black replied, a little condescendingly, "this is why you have us."

"I don't have you. Or at least, I didn't hire you. They're right about that," Fin said, jerking his head toward the three Intrepid people across the table. "You took it upon yourself to jump on this. You probably saw dollar signs being flushed down your own toilet when someone else wanted to adapt my book."

Whitson fidgeted and cleared his throat, but Fin cut him off.

"Yes," he said, his eyes a little wild by now, "it's my book. Anybody who has read *DragonCache* could see that. And while I think you're right that Universal doesn't have the right to sue you over that, *I* certainly do.

"As the author, I'm ultimately the one who gets to decide who can adapt my book into a movie, or even if this whole thing goes to court at all." He turned back toward Black. "I like Intrepid's screenplay, even though it was obviously plagiarized from my book."

It was Marion Plum's turn to fidget, and she looked a little embarrassed. She lifted her hands and buried her face in them.

"Ms. Plum," Fin continued, "I don't want to point too many fingers. I know you wrote the screenplay, and it was obviously based on my book, but I figure the order ultimately came down from Mr. Whitson, anyway.

"That being said, I'm not necessarily looking to sue Mr. Whitson or Intrepid Studios, either." He took a moment to take a breath as the others looked at each other, some curiously, some timorously.

"As the author," Fin said, "I know that I have the right to sell Intrepid Studios the right to adapt my book for the screen." Black looked a little nervous and embarrassed and he glanced across the table at Whitson. "The hard work there has already been done," Fin continued. "As I said, I like the screenplay. All I ask is that the names be changed back to the names that I created for the characters. And give me credit for the original story."

"How much are we talking about here?" Whitson asked apprehensively.

"I don't know," Fin replied with a glance at Daryl. "That would be up to the proverbial bean counters."

"The problem is," Whitson continued in a low, breathless tone that seemed to indicate that he knew he'd been beaten, "we have a pretty limited budget. I'm still trying to raise capital."

"Okay, well what if Intrepid and Universal work together on this? I could sell Universal the right to distribute the movie. They could put up some capital, maybe even use their clout to bring in some bigger names to star in it than you could manage.

"I mean, I don't know for certain how all that works, but I always see multiple production company logos at the beginning of movies, in association with some big, well-known studio. So, I know we can pull this off."

"Look, son," Black started, sounding a little exasperated, but Fin interrupted him.

"No, *you* look. Mr. Black, I've gotten pretty fed up with your bluster and your condescension. You started out viewing Intrepid Studios as the enemy, and I admit I was a little pissed, too, when I saw that they had stolen my story and claimed it as their own. While I don't want to reward bad behavior, I also don't want to miss out on something that could benefit, well, me certainly, but lots of others as well. Including Universal.

"But Mr. Black, you were just so focused on throwing your weight around, you've wasted two days, now, scaring the shit out of these people because you think they stole a potential moneymaker from you. But they didn't. They stole it from *me*.

"Now we have a chance here to make this right. I've always thought that *DragonCache* was blockbuster material, and now, here's someone who wants to make it. I don't want Universal standing in the way of that. I'd be perfectly happy signing on with Paramount or Warner Brothers. But because of *TimePlex* and *A Place Made of Time*, I'm giving Universal first chance."

Fin took a deep breath as his eyes bored into Randall Black.

"So, I say put up or shut up."

It might have only been a few seconds, but it seemed like minutes passed in complete silence until two or three people nervously cleared their throats. Finally, Daryl leaned forward and glanced at Fin with a raised eyebrow and his lips shaped into a grin.

"Gentlemen," he said, "and Ms. Plum, what Mr. Jones has suggested certainly seems doable." Black stirred a little next to him, but Daryl raised his hand toward him and acknowledged his anticipated objection. "Yes, it's certainly more complicated than the way he stated it, but we can do this.

"Let me get together with a couple of people and I'll draft a few details. Then, we can meet back here tomorrow and see if we can nail it down. I mean if everyone is in agreement about going this route?"

He looked briefly at each face in the room. All nodded their assent, though Black and Whitson seemed to do so a little begrudgingly.

"Very good," Daryl concluded. "Well, I think this took a surprising but welcome turn."

Sitting in the restaurant now, with a satisfied smile on his face, Fin swallowed the last of his wine. He couldn't wait to see the details that would be presented tomorrow.

The only thing that would make this evening better would be Suzy sitting across from me.

26

Mark came back on Monday to get his things. He had rent-
ed a small truck and was accompanied by Steve. Michelle
was there since she didn't work on Mondays, and she
wanted to talk it out.

"I'll go out and get the blankets and the dolly out of the
truck," Steve said quietly and excused himself.

"I don't know what else there is to say," Mark said after Steve
had gone outside.

"I fucked up, Mark," Michelle implored, "I know that. But
breaking old habits, isn't that bound to happen?"

"Maybe so. I'm just not prepared to stand by and welcome
you back after all of your setbacks."

"But Mark, we love each other." How could he not see how
important that was?

"I think I was being a little too ambitious when I agreed to
help you through this," he said, ignoring her statement, "or a
little too confident in my own abilities. My stupid Mr. Fix-it nature stepped up and told me I could do this." He shook his head.
"The coke was bad enough. But then there's the alcohol." His
voice became more bitter. "And, apparently, your addiction to
fucking other men."

Michelle's eyes were stinging now with the rising tears.

"You're the only one that means anything to me."

Mark scoffed at the statement.

"Lucky me. You're out there fucking every Tom, Dick and
Harry, but at least I have the satisfaction of knowing that I'm the
one you care about."

"Mark, I love you so much," Michelle cried. "I'm so sorry!"

"I'm sorry, too, Michelle. But I feel like I'm the personifica-
tion of Nietzsche's aphorism. When I'm with you, it's like I'm
gazing into the abyss." Michelle wasn't sure what that meant,
but she kept quiet, waiting for him to continue. He took a deep,

shaky breath, his eyes cast downward. "I feel like it's starting to look back, now, and I can't just stick around and wait for it to suck me in."

He looked up at her and shook his head.

"I'm sorry, I just can't do it anymore." He glanced around and sighed. "I need to go get Steve so we can get started." He turned and left Michelle standing there.

Feeling an intense sadness and anxiety descending over her, she went up to the bedroom and snorted a couple of bumps, the last ones in her last 8 ball. She felt better almost immediately, but she forced herself to stay there for a little while to let her emotions even out a bit.

Since her house was already fully furnished, Mark had put a number of his things in storage when he moved in, so there wasn't much for him to get.

When she came back downstairs, Mark was gone.

Her chemically induced alacrity combined with the very real sadness and disappointment made her feel confused. The return of her blinding headache didn't help, nor did the fatigue. But she figured it was just her recent inactivity. She had been so down lately and had gotten very little exercise. Not even any sex for weeks.

Okay, she remembered that she couldn't say that about the sex anymore. But that one time just primed the pump and made her feel the need even more.

She decided she needed to go out.

§

The interior of the club was throbbing with the beat of the dance music, colored lights flashing this way and that. Michelle didn't hear the melody so much as she felt the pulse of the music beating through her body. It was as if the DJ knew exactly what she needed.

The dating site would take time. This was more immediate. She was glad to be back. She didn't realize when she was with Mark that she missed this. Mark wasn't into clubbing, and when she was with him, Michelle was happy to give it up. But she realized now that it almost felt like coming home. It felt comfortable, familiar.

145

Still, she was a little anxious. She had come with an agenda. Mark had broken her heart. Yes, she knew it was ultimately her own fuck-up that had caused it, but Mark just couldn't understand her issues, not like he said he did. If he had, he would have been more sympathetic. He would have known that she couldn't go that long without it. It was almost as if he had purposely doomed her to failure.

So, she needed to break free of him. She had to guarantee that she would get laid. Therefore, she wore the most provocative outfit she could come up with, a narrow sparkly tube top and the shortest skirt she owned. She didn't bother trying to pull it down to cover the crease below her butt cheeks. That would be defeating the purpose.

The small hits of cocaine she had taken earlier had worn off, and with Mark gone, she had felt the depression settling over her big time. So, she called Candy to get some more, meeting him on the way to the club. He had raised his eyebrows and licked his lips when he saw how she was dressed, but she was too focused on getting the drugs to realize it until later. She purchased a full gram this time – much more expensive, but a better value than buying an 8 ball at a time.

A couple of lines and she was ready to hit the club.

Once she was on the floor, though, she felt the anxiety dissipating a little. She wasn't actually looking for anyone, but several were looking at her. She was just on the dance floor, alone, letting the music move her.

She was surprised to feel tears on her cheeks. Not tears of sadness, she was sure of that. They were tears of relief at being back in her element.

She felt as if she had come home.

It didn't take long for him to show up. She didn't know him, but she knew his type. He had dark hair, slicked back, dark eyes and a slim manicured mustache and goatee. He wore a shiny silvery blazer and a silver ring in each earlobe.

She'd had her eyes closed as she moved to the music, and when she opened them, he was in front of her, dancing with her. Michelle smiled. He would do just fine.

"Why were you crying?" he asked.

"Crying?" Michelle looked at him. He glanced up at her across the bar in his living room.

"When I first saw you on the dance floor, you were crying."

She sighed as she thought about her answer. They had spent a few minutes dancing before they decided to retire to the bar. They each had a drink, and he produced a little packet of pills. It had been ages since she had taken ecstasy, and she was loving it.

"Not really crying," she finally replied. "I just broke up with my boyfriend, and he was never into clubs. I'd forgotten how much I loved it."

He lived just a block away from the club, and he had suggested they come here to get away from the noise. He put the cap back on the bottle of Jameson and picked up the glasses. He handed one to Michelle, and she took a sip.

"Mark drank Jameson," she said.

"Mark?" he asked.

"My ex-boyfriend." She felt a twinge uttering the phrase, but she resolutely pushed it aside.

He nodded and frowned. He took a drink, then set his glass down on the coffee table in front of his sofa. He sat down and grabbed her hand, pulling her down next to him.

Sitting down, her tiny skirt didn't even cover her panties, but she didn't bother trying to pull it down. She had an agenda, after all.

He put his arm around her shoulders, placing his other hand on her thigh. Leaning in, he kissed her as his hand crept higher. It took only a couple of moves for his hand to be between her legs, pressing against her.

She remembered Mark taking his time. He had admitted once that he was probably still rushing it more than some women would like. But he acknowledged that he tried to take it slow, to allow her time to get in the mood.

She was pretty much in the mood the moment Mark looked at her 'that way.' She hadn't admitted that to him, though, because she found that she liked the slow approach, the foreplay. With

Mark, it was more than just the fucking. It was lovemaking, and it was always good.

"My ex used to work up to that slowly," she said quietly, almost cautiously.

He pulled his face away to look her in the eyes.

"Mark?" he asked. Michelle nodded, then she shook her head.

"I'm sorry. I need to shut up about him."

"Yeah, the motherfucker's not even here and he's spoiling the mood."

"Sorry," she repeated, and she leaned back in to kiss him.

She could feel that she was wet where his hand was pressing, and she desperately wanted to feel his fingers on her clit, the way Mark used to do.

She had realized months before that a good number of the men she had been with didn't seem to know about the clitoris, and several of those who did spent very little time there. A surprising number didn't even seem to know what to do with it. It was either that they only wanted to selfishly satisfy their own desires, or else they just didn't really think about hers.

"Could you," she started hesitantly, "maybe massage my clit a little?"

Again, he pulled away and looked at her.

"Let me guess," he said, his voice sounding a little exasperated, "Mark?"

Michelle looked at him a little cautiously.

"I . . ." she whispered, "I just like it."

He stared at her for a few moments, then sighed.

"Fine," he said, pushing her skirt up. He slipped his hand down the front of her panties and began impatiently rubbing his finger up and down on her clit. To Michelle, it felt almost abrasive, not at all like lovemaking.

"Softly," she said, "and slowly."

"Oh, for fuck's sake!" he exclaimed. He pulled his hand out of her panties and grabbed her tube top, pulling it down. The seam ripped apart, sending sequins flying in all directions.

He pinched her nipple and yanked her closer, kissing her almost violently. Michelle felt the tears coming again and, trying to purge her memories of Mark, she reached between his legs. Through his pants, she could feel him already hard and erect.

She felt ashamed when she heard herself whimper, realizing how much she had lost. But feeling his hand on her breast, she knew she was about to get what she needed right now. She just had to forfeit what she wanted.

27

Michelle smiled and said goodbye as her client walked out of the salon. The smile disappeared as soon as the client was out of sight. She had forced it because that's what you do. Now, it required too much effort.

Mark had been gone for a month now, and Michelle had settled back into her old routines. The drinking, drugs and sex felt, well, not necessarily good, but it was familiar and welcoming. And depressing.

Her headache and fatigue had returned, as they did most days. She knew that depression could manifest itself with physical symptoms, and today, those symptoms had pulled out all the stops. She collapsed in the chair, knowing she didn't have another client for a half hour. She just needed to rest.

"Michelle."

Hearing her name spoken in such a sharp tone jerked her awake. She didn't realize that she had fallen asleep in the chair, but she came fully awake when she saw the alarmed expression on the face of Sheree, the salon's receptionist.

"What?" Michelle asked, feeling even more exhausted after her unexpected nap. "What is it?"

"Your 3:00 is here," Sheree replied, "but I think you should go home."

"Why?" Michelle looked around, feeling a little disoriented.

"You don't look good." Sheree put her hand on the side of Michelle's face. "Oh my god, you feel like you're burning up, and –" her hand touched just a little below Michelle's jaw, "girl, you got some serious glands here. I think you got the flu."

"I'll be alright. I just have a couple more clients, then I'll go home and get some rest."

"Uh uh," Sheree shook her head, "you don't need to be getting your clients sick. Or us. We'll reschedule them, or someone else can take them. You get your ass home now."

Michelle didn't feel like she had the strength to argue with Sheree, much less to stand on her feet for another two hours. She nodded and pushed herself up out of the chair. Sheree headed back to the front counter to take care of Paula, Michelle's 3:00, while Michelle gathered up her things, feeling as if she was moving through molasses.

"I'm so sorry," she said to Paula as she walked toward the front door. Paula shook her head, and waved it off, her face etched with sympathy.

"Oh, honey, please don't worry about it. Just feel better."

§

Michelle felt a little better, or at least, she felt a little calmer. On her drive home, she had felt so bad that she stopped at an urgent care facility. The doctor agreed that her symptoms were, indeed, fairly severe, but as there were still a few cases of flu being reported, he recommended drinking lots of liquids and getting lots of rest. As a precaution, though, they took some blood and sent it to their lab for testing.

So, while she still felt like shit, she also felt a little relieved that it wasn't something more serious. That relief went away, though, just two days later when the doctor called her and asked her to come back in. He wouldn't tell her why, so she worried all the way there.

As she sat, fully-clothed this time, on the examination table, she didn't feel any better as she watched the doctor gazing at her file. As he was looking at it, Michelle's mind was swirling turbulently, thinking about the men she had been with. Alcohol and/or drugs were almost always involved, and she seldom had full control of her faculties. But she did remember that at least one of the men hadn't used a condom. What the hell was she going to do with a baby?

"What is it, doctor?" Michelle finally asked. He glanced at her, then back at the file. He sighed, cleared his throat, then placed the file on the counter, sitting up straight to look at her.

"The lab ran tests on the blood we drew a couple of days ago." Michelle nodded. "I'm afraid there are some complications that I hadn't foreseen."

"Complications?" Michelle echoed. "How complicated? Is it twins? Triplets? What?"

"What?" The doctor seemed surprised by her question, but he shook his head. "No, I'm sorry, it's nothing like that." He took a deep, fortifying breath and looked Michelle squarely in the face. "I'm afraid you're HIV-positive."

Michelle felt as if she had been punched in the gut. A few seconds passed before she could take a breath, and even then, it wasn't a very deep one.

"I have AIDS?" she asked weakly.

"No," the doctor replied quickly, shaking his head. "You have HIV. HIV is the virus that causes AIDS, but you're not at that point now. Not even close. In fact, these flu symptoms you've been experiencing are actually encouraging. It means we may have caught it in its very early stages. With treatment, it's entirely possible that you can live a long, healthy life."

"I'm HIV-positive. How the fuck can I be healthy?"

"It's a common misconception that a lot of people have." The doctor's tone was calming. "Effective antiretroviral medications have been available for a while now. HIV is certainly not always fatal. And again, with treatment, it's possible it may never even progress to AIDS."

Michelle sat there a few moments, wishing that person with the sledgehammer would back away from her head. The doctor lifted the cover of the folder, looking at her file again.

"It says here that you're not married. Do you have a partner?"

Michelle scoffed.

"What day is it?"

"Multiple partners?"

Michelle nodded.

"Well," he continued quietly, "I'm required by law to notify the health department when someone tests positive for HIV. Shortly after that, they'll be contacting you to discuss notifying your partners so they can get tested, as well."

Michelle leaned forward, her elbows resting on her knees, her face in her hands. She couldn't even remember most of their names.

"I think the first thing we should do, though, is to discuss treatment options." The doctor pulled a couple of pamphlets out of the folder and started talking about the drugs that were available, but by this time, it sounded like static to Michelle.

28

Suzy jerked as she snapped awake, looking around completely flustered for a few moments. She had drifted off to sleep in the chair after the last episode, and she felt confused and disoriented until she remembered where she was.

As the last episodes seeped back into her mind, Suzy felt emotionally drained, drenched in the overwhelming sadness of Michelle's dreary life. She couldn't help hoping the best for Michelle, even though she already knew, from Joan, how it turned out for her.

She wiped her face and felt the crust of dried tears on the side of her face. The tears had just kept coming last night when she finished the episodes, partly at having seen Mark for what she knew would be the last time, and partly over the crushing diagnosis that the doctor had delivered to Michelle.

She straightened up in the chair, rotating her neck to get the kinks out. She was surprised to find that Michelle took up the majority of her concentration, rather than Mark. She was ashamed to remember how she used to think about Michelle, with expressions like slut or party girl. She had no idea what Michelle had been going through until now, the overwhelming physical and psychological pull of her addictions, the utter helplessness against the magnetic seduction they held over her.

She took a breath and shook her head, resolved to try to be more empathetic. She couldn't know what others were going through until, as the saying goes, she walked a mile in their shoes.

She looked at her watch. It was after 5:00. She had slept through the night. Yet she hadn't experienced any of the screaming or other disruptions that Joan had complained about.

Still, despite several hours of sleep, she felt exhausted, completely depleted. She heaved a heavy sigh and stretched as she looked around. Creeped out by the feeling of being watched earlier in the evening, she had pulled the drapes closed, and the room was especially dark. But she smelled a hint of incense. Sandalwood.

She stood up, pushed the drapes open and saw the first shafts of sunrise as they began chasing the shadows away. She knew she needed to get home, even if it was only for a few minutes.

She felt guilty leaving Ursula all alone in the fenced backyard area behind her house. She knew the little dog had shelter and water, and the overnight July temperature was comfortable enough. But Ursula was a house dog, accustomed to being with her people. She wasn't used to being left alone outside.

With traffic driving into the sun, the half-hour trip took longer than usual. A couple of times, she thought she saw that old grey Honda in her rear-view mirror again. But watching the mirror longer than she should have, she wandered into the next lane, almost hitting a BMW in the process.

She knew she was being silly. Again, it was probably just Michelle's paranoia bleeding over into her own consciousness.

Besides the apparent paranoia, the depression settling over her was profound, and she knew she had to do something to break loose from it. She felt, emotionally, almost as if she was right back where she had been when Mark and Emma died over four years ago.

She punched the button on the radio and remembered Michelle turning on her radio exactly the same way after her indiscretion with Joaquin. *Good Riddance* by Green Day was playing. *That won't do it,* Suzy thought. She pressed a button for a different station. *Uptown Funk* was playing on this station. That's better. An upbeat song was what she needed. It was full daylight by the time she got home.

When she opened the back door, Ursula jumped and let out a little bark of alarm as she lifted her head. When she saw it was Suzy, she was instantly on her feet, bouncing up and down at the fence, and Suzy couldn't help but smile, her eyes stinging.

She opened the gate and knelt as Ursula jumped enthusiastically into her lap. Suzy wrapped her arms around the little dog and wept.

§

Feeling generous and magnanimous, and admittedly a little guilty, Suzy decided that Ursula deserved more than just a couple of minutes of her time and a bowl of food. She clipped the leash onto her collar and took her for a walk around the neighborhood, hoping that the activity outside would help to elevate her own mood, as well.

Oh no, she thought as she saw Terri, her fifty-something, super-religious neighbor walking toward her, her hope of lifting her spirits plummeting. Terri had offered the services of her priest a few years ago when a local paper had published, against Suzy's wishes, a story about Fiona, the ghost in Suzy's carriage house. Suzy had declined, while barely keeping her snark in check.

With the state she was in this morning, Suzy was afraid she might bring down the wrath of God on her if she allowed herself to fully engage. But it was too late. Terri looked up and saw her, and pasted on a stiff smile as a greeting.

Suzy wasn't usually out in the neighborhood this early, or ever, so she hadn't seen Terri since that time at her door a few years before, except in passing, in her car, fortunately. A polite wave was easy enough to pull off at those times. Now, unfortunately, she was going to have to actually be civilized.

"Good morning," Terri said. Her smile looked a little more genuine when she looked down at Ursula. "I didn't know you had a Pomeranian."

Suzy was surprised at the feeling that came over her. Benevolence? Compassion? That was completely unexpected, but she recalled the feeling she had felt an hour or so before in relation to Michelle, and her resolve to be more empathetic.

"Good morning, Terri," she said with a smile that, she was surprised to find, actually felt genuine. "Yes, she's Fin's dog." Terri stopped and knelt to pet Ursula, cooing in that voice that people usually use when talking to little dogs. Suddenly, Suzy felt a little more kinship toward her neighbor.

Dammit!

"I had two little Pomeranians a few years ago. So sweet and cheerful."

"Yes, she's a little lover, alright," Suzy smiled.

"What's her name?" Terri asked.

"Ursula."

Terri looked up at her with a look of surprise.

"What an unusual name for a cute little dog," she said.

"Fin named her after one of his favorite writers. And the name means 'little bear' so, considering the way she looks, he thought it fit."

"Well, yes, it does, yes it sure does," Terri said to Ursula, continuing with 'the voice.' The little dog didn't seem to mind at all.

Terri looked up at Suzy while still petting Ursula and, to Suzy's relief, changed to her normal voice.

"How have you been?"

"Fine. Doing really well." Suzy nodded, kind of flustered, casting about for something a little deeper to say. "Fin and I are engaged."

"Congratulations. That's great." Terri's voice wasn't exactly saturated with enthusiasm, but neither was it cold or critical. And in Suzy's effort to be more empathetic, she admitted to herself that she wasn't one to get overly enthusiastic, either.

Terri stood up.

"I understand your ghost is gone now."

Suzy wasn't sure how to read her motive. There was no real tone in her voice. Not a question, just a simple statement.

"Yes, she is. She moved on a few years ago." Suzy decided not to volunteer the news of her continued contact with other spirits.

"That's good," Terri nodded, seeming a little lost for words herself. They came, hesitantly, a few seconds later. "You know, back when I came to your door, I never meant to come off as so . . ." She paused, trying to think of the word.

"Judgmental?" Suzy volunteered.

Terri's face expressed momentary shock, possibly even offense, Suzy was fiendishly happy to note. But the surprise eased after a couple of seconds.

"Yes, I suppose that's a good word," Terri nodded ruefully. "I didn't mean to come across as so judgmental. That article in the Salem paper just made it sound so scary and pagan."

"It's Salem," Suzy said with a shrug. "Scary and pagan is their bread and butter."

"Yeah, I guess you're right," Terri replied with a smile. "Anyway, I'm sorry if I sounded that way to you. I probably wouldn't have reacted very well myself if the tables were turned. And I'm sorry it's taken me this long to apologize."

Suzy shook her head dismissively and smiled.

"It's okay. But I appreciate that. And I'm sorry if I said anything to exacerbate the situation."

Terri nodded and her smile seemed more sincere.

For some reason, Suzy remembered her visit with Lilith. God, was that just yesterday?

"Terri," she began before she could stop it, "I wonder if you could do me a favor."

Terri looked at her apprehensively, as if she was afraid to commit to anything yet. Before she had the chance to back down, Suzy plunged forward.

"Would you be able to take me out on the harbor sometime soon?"

Terri looked at her, a frown of confusion deeply etched on her face.

"I know that's kind of an unusual request," Suzy continued, "but I don't really know any other neighbors very well. I'm an introvert, and tend to keep to myself, so . . ." She left the thought hanging for a moment, then decided that a little further explanation was called for.

"As you know, I don't have a boat anymore." Her voice was quiet, as she knew everyone was aware of her story. "I see you taking your boat out every now and then." *Come on, out with it.*

"Okay, a friend recommended that I visit the site of the accident, where Mark and Emma died. For closure, you know? To," she hesitated, almost gritting her teeth, "to make my peace with the Lord." She didn't know if that's how religious people still talked, but it seemed to have a positive effect on Terri.

"Oh," Terri replied, breathily. "Of course. I'd be happy to." Tears actually came to Suzy's eyes at Terri's response. *God dammit!*

"Thanks, Terri. Maybe sometime this evening, if you're available then?"

"Absolutely. Just let me know."

"I will. Thank you so much."

Suzy glanced at her watch, and Terri spoke up before she did.

"Yeah, I need to get going, myself. But it was good talking with you."

"You too."

"And give me a call. I'll be happy to take you out on my boat."

What the hell was that? Suzy thought as she walked away. *I wonder if this means we're going to be friends, now.*

§

The drive back to Joan's place was uneventful, though she knew she had her eyes in the rear-view mirror more often than usual.

She felt a little safer, though. As soon as she got home, Suzy had made a stop at a cabinet in a room near the back door that was used as the mud room. The cabinet held a collection of items like keys and charger cables and other things that most people, she knew, kept in what they referred to as their junk drawer.

Suzy wasn't sure what it meant that she had a cabinet for this stuff instead of just a drawer.

A few years before, during a time of political upheaval, when dangerous racially charged or gender-based confrontations were frighteningly common, Fin had gotten her a stun gun. She hated the idea of even having it, but she appreciated his concern.

Now, whether it was real or just paranoia, she felt like she needed some protection. She had pressed the button and, after all the time it had spent in the cabinet, it barely made a spark, so she plugged it in to charge while she walked Ursula.

After depositing the little dog, grumpily, back in her quarters outside, Suzy picked up the stun gun and pressed the button. This time, it crackled loudly, a blue-white electric arc flashing between the two metal contacts.

The sound made her jump as it always did, but that was the point, wasn't it? She unplugged the charge cable and dropped the stun gun in her purse.

29

Ｈow's it going?" Suzy was driving back to Saugus after walking Ursula and having her completely unexpected conversation with Terri, when Joan called her before work.

"It's going well," Suzy replied. She didn't want to go into too much detail, especially about Mark, but she had been putting her off for too long. "I've just seen the episode where the doctor diagnosed Michelle with HIV. I don't know how many more episodes Michelle wants to show me, but I may be finished today. I can't imagine there will be very much more to see after this."

"Wait," Joan said, "you mean you really see what she saw?"

"I really do, Joan. Didn't I explain that to you?"

"Yeah, you did," Joan replied, sounding a little bewildered. "I guess I still didn't really believe in it."

"Yes, I see every memory she cares to show me."

"Wow." A few quiet seconds passed. "Was there any screaming or anything like that last night?"

"No, all was quiet."

"Huh. Okay. Well, I guess I'll just wait to hear back from you."

"Sounds good, Joan. I'll definitely let you know when I've seen everything Michelle wants to show me."

As she disconnected and placed her phone down on the passenger seat, she felt that prickly sensation again. She looked in the rear view mirror, and both side mirrors. She didn't see anyone obviously following her, but she knew she was no Jason Bourne, either. Maybe she was just being paranoid.

§

Shit! Michelle thought as she slowly left the salon. She realized that she had forgotten to take her medication again.

She had mixed feelings about the medication. She often experienced diarrhea and nausea as a result of it, not to mention the almost constant headache. When she forgot it, as she had today, the side-effects were seldom an issue. Especially was that the case when she forgot multiple days in a row.

She did remember to take her medication when she was sick with the latest respiratory infection or head cold or any number of other random infections that had begun afflicting her. But once she kicked that, it was easy to forget again.

Michelle didn't like thinking about the fact that the infections were becoming more frequent. Too often, when a fever would appear out of nowhere, she had to shuffle clients, or refer them to one of the other cosmetologists in the salon. She was seeing fewer clients now so that she could schedule rest times between appointments. It was starting to get bad enough that some clients had already switched to other stylists.

Still, she was able to manage. Her HIV medication was costly, though it cost less when she didn't take it. She was more inclined to take her recreational drugs, which were also costly. But she had no house payment, thanks to Mark, one more thing that occasionally brought him to mind after all this time. He hadn't demanded that she pay him back, and her abundant accumulation of guilt included that, as well.

Over the last few years, since she lost Mark, she had resettled into her old routine of drugs, drinking, clubbing and one-night-stands. It wasn't satisfying, but it was familiar. And it felt better than the diarrhea, nausea and headaches. Was it any wonder the new medication agenda was difficult to settle into?

At first, she was surprised at how few men were turned off by her HIV-positive status. When she told them, as she was required by law, there was usually a bit of hesitation. But if she was willing, so were they, usually. They slipped on a condom and got down to it.

Last night was no exception. Although it had taken longer than it had in the past. In fact, she realized, that had been the

162

case for the last several months. She didn't like to admit it, but she knew she wasn't looking as good as she used to. Her face was a little more drawn and now required a bit more cosmetic enhancement before she felt comfortable going out.

She was skinny, though. She liked that. A few years before, when she had gotten off the drugs, with Mark's help, she was always ravenous. She felt as if she couldn't get enough to eat, and she felt as if it showed. Now, keeping the weight off wasn't a problem at all. But it seemed as if some guys liked a more voluptuous figure than she possessed now.

But eventually, someone would always be interested.

She didn't remember his name. She seldom did. But last night was fairly unremarkable. As usual, she started out dancing alone, usually with some blow and some alcohol in her system. She didn't have many friends anymore. But as she swayed in time to the music, all that her diminished energy and chronic pain allowed these days, eventually someone, responding to her short skirt or her bouncing boobs or her seductive moves, always ended up in front of her. And she usually ended up going home with them, or vice versa.

Sometimes, if she was especially missing Mark, or missing the kind of intimacy that she had shared with him those years ago, she might want them to stay together through the night. That feeling usually wasn't reciprocated, though. Last night, Michelle made sure that she had plenty of liquor on hand, in a wide variety, snacks, etc.

But what's-his-name made do with one drink before he started stripping down. A few minutes later, when they were finished, Michelle offered a nightcap, but he declined, donning his clothing almost as quickly as he had doffed them.

After he left, Michelle treated herself to what she had offered him, followed by another, and another. It was no wonder she hadn't remembered, this morning, to take her medication.

Although the headache she had when she woke up could have served as a reminder.

Sadly, she didn't feel like going out and indulging her whims and addictions as often as she used to. With the random illnesses and general low energy level that frequently afflicted her, she experienced minor withdrawal symptoms more often than she wanted to admit.

As she took a weary breath and walked away from the salon onto the sidewalk, she saw a familiar figure ahead.

"Mark?" she called. He turned, and Michelle's heart flipped.

"Michelle," he said after a couple of seconds' hesitation. In those seconds, Michelle saw the wheels turning as he tried to place her. She knew she didn't look the same as she did when they were together. Still, he smiled graciously.

"How are you doing, Mark?" she asked, her whole body quivering in his presence.

"I'm doing well . . . And you?" Again, she caught the brief hesitation before he asked about her health.

"Fine. It's so good to see you."

"You, too," Mark replied, with a genuine smile. Michelle wasn't sure if it was entirely a feeling of goodwill, or if there was some sympathy mixed with it. She saw that a lot lately.

"What are you doing around here?"

"I'm on my way to a business meeting." He shrugged. "Trying to sell my latest project." He smiled, and Michelle remembered back when he would talk to her about what he was working on, sharing his life with her. She remembered the intimacy of her life with Mark, not just the physical intimacy but emotional. The closeness, the affectionate touches, the glances, and her eyes misted over.

"I've never stopped thinking of you," she said, shaking her head. She took a deep breath. "Do you ever . . ." She stopped, shaking her head, knowing how hokey she was about to sound. What she said next, she realized, was no better. "Do you think you might like to give us another go?"

"Well," Mark said, pausing for a moment, "I'm married, now. I married Suzy Drummond. We have a little girl, Emma." The smile that took over his face at the mention of his wife and daughter eclipsed any that she had ever seen when she had been with him. Forcing a smile, the mist in her eyes turned into a full wall of water.

"Oh, Mark," she said while trying not to choke on the words, "I'm so happy for you."

"Thanks," Mark replied, touching her elbow briefly, and she felt that old electricity that was so common before she had lost him. "I really do have to go, though," he said, glancing at his watch. "I'm late."

"Of course," Michelle nodded, but she made a point of grabbing his arm as she looked him deeply in his eyes. In that brief moment, she saw all the lost looks, all the missed touches, all the yearned-for kisses. She saw the entire weight of her regret in what she had forfeited with Mark, and it felt like a knife in her heart. "It was so good to see you again."

"You too," Mark said, his smile fully sympathetic, now.

"Tell Suzy I said hi."

"I will. Thanks."

As she watched him walk away, looking for the door he needed for his business meeting, the tears in Michelle's eyes spilled over and cascaded down her cheeks. Through the tears, she finally managed to find her way to her car and collapsed into it, giving full vent to her bitter emotions.

§

Suzy came out of the episode, her body taut and tense. She picked up her cup. The tea was still warm.

She barely remembered that day, when Mark told her that he had seen Michelle. A trivial comment tossed out as they worked on dinner together. Although she remembered that his next remark was less than trivial.

"She really looked like shit. She looked sick."

She couldn't remember if they had discussed Michelle or her appearance after that, or if they had moved on to some other more pleasant subject. Like Emma's play date with Amber, the little girl on the next block, or what they were going to do that weekend, or maybe their upcoming vacation to Walt Disney World.

Michelle was in the past, forgotten and cast aside. Hardly a blip on their radar.

165

Swallowing the last of her tea, Suzy put the cup down, feeling the shame suffuse her whole being.

30

Michelle lay on a bed with just a sheet over her as she struggled to open her eyes. She had never felt so exhausted, but she couldn't remember where she was. What was his name?

There was an unfamiliar sound nearby. Did he have a white noise machine? She couldn't even place his face. In fact, the face that came to mind was Debra, a client.

Then, she remembered. She had been at the salon. She had just finished with Debra, a dye job and perm for her daughter's wedding next month, when Michelle felt the pain and fatigue wash over her in a rush. She also felt sudden chills, as if she had a high fever.

But that was the last thing she remembered.

She remembered things before that, though. She recalled that she had stopped going out to the clubs. And, unfortunately, she remembered the last man she took home. Particularly, she remembered the look on his face as she undressed, and he saw the sores that lined her vulva. Even with a condom, he decided he wasn't interested.

So, her original struggle to remember who she was with was just a memory fragment from an earlier time. It apparently had nothing to do with where she was now.

It was just as well. By that time, she had already reduced her club and sex time to weekends only. Even at that, she seldom had the stamina for it and often opted to stay home, wallowing in her depression.

Now, her life consisted of little more than resting at home and working when she felt up to it.

Putting forth a great effort, she managed to lift her eyelids. She was lying on her back, looking up at a grid of white suspended ceiling tiles. It took several seconds for the pattern to become recognizable as a ceiling. But where was she?

She turned her head a little to the right, toward the sound she heard, a drone and a beeping sound, and she realized it sounded nothing like a white noise machine. She saw the monitor with multicolored lines and numbers showing her blood pressure, heart rate, blood oxygen and temperature. She frowned, trying to make sense of it.

She sensed a slight movement on the other side, and she laboriously turned her head back to the left. Someone was sitting there, but they were farther away than the monitor had been. It seemed as if it took a few moments for her eyes to find the correct distance and to come into focus. Then, the shape turned into her mother's face.

"Oh, shit," she said as she slipped again into merciful unconsciousness.

§

"Rise and shine, baby girl," Joan said as Michelle's eyes tentatively opened. The hospital bed had been elevated, so she wasn't flat on her back any longer. She felt a little stronger now, but she experienced a feeling of nausea when she saw her mother's face near her. And the sour stench of her whiskey breath didn't help.

Joan leaned over and hugged Michelle.

"What the fuck are you doing here?" Michelle asked, her voice sodden with fatigue. She knew the weariness she felt was more than just physical.

"Well, is that any way to talk to your long-lost mama?" She backed away and plopped back down in the vinyl-covered chair, grinning at the farting noise it made.

"Seriously, mother, what the fuck are you doing here?"

"Dammit, Michelle, can't you call me Mom?"

"Mother!"

Joan chuckled.

"I guess you never thought to change the emergency contacts on your file. Still going to Dr. Conrad, huh? God, he must be in his seventies by now."

Michelle rolled her eyes with disgust at her own stupid negligence, and when her eyelids closed, it felt good enough that she was tempted to keep them that way, especially with her mother

168

there. But she wanted to know what happened. She opened her eyes again and took in her surroundings, then focused on her mother.

"What happened?"

"I guess you took quite a spill at your salon. I didn't know you'd become a hair stylist. Good for you, baby girl. Anyway, from what they told me, you were finishing up with a customer, then you just toppled down onto the floor.

"Honey, why didn't you tell me you have AIDS? I would have made it a point to come around sooner."

"You just answered your own question."

"Oh, Michelle, when are you going to stop thinking of me as the devil?"

"I don't. I don't want to insult the devil."

"Ha! That's a good one." Joan's smile quickly faded. "You ungrateful little bitch."

"Ungrateful?" Michelle's anger propelled her a little more upright, and the monitor began beeping faster. Her frailty, however, quickly made her collapse back onto the bed again, breathing heavily. "You treated Nicky and me like shit and expect me to be grateful?"

"You poor little sensitive baby. I never realized you were so delicate. I didn't treat you like shit."

"If you weren't at work, you were usually drunk. And you were a fucking mean drunk. Me and Nicky, we both learned at an early age how much it hurts to be backhanded by our own mother.

"And if we threatened to tell anyone the true story of how we got a black eye or a bloody nose or a bruise on our cheek, instead of the lies you made up, you turned on the tears. 'Oh, I'm so sorry. I didn't mean to do that. It won't happen again.' But it always did. Usually within only a day or two."

"Do you have any idea how much trouble you and Nicky were? Both of you gave me shit every day." Joan's eyes took on a sheen as they filled with tears.

The door opened and a nurse came in, looking at the monitor. Joan wiped a tear from her eye as the nurse looked at her. The nurse looked at Michelle and noticed her elevated breathing was slowing again.

"Try not to get too excited," the nurse advised, placing a hand on Michelle's arm. "Your body's in a weakened state. You need to rest."

"I tried to tell her that," Joan sighed with an exasperated shake of her head, her voice sounding pained, as if she was at the end of her rope with her rebellious daughter. Michelle shot her a look of pure anger and hatred. The nurse was making an adjustment to the monitor and didn't see Michelle's reaction. She glanced at Joan and Michelle again, then turned and left the room.

Joan looked at Michelle and shook her head.

"Jesus, baby girl, you're such a petite little flower. You seriously need to grow a thicker skin."

"Kids shouldn't need a thick skin to deal with their mother." Michelle's voice was growing weaker. "Seriously, mother, why are you here? Just because the doctor called you, you finally show up? You don't seem terribly torn up by my condition, so why? You haven't been around for years."

"You're right," Joan replied, "I haven't been around for years. I moved to Florida with Joe."

"Joe?"

"You didn't know him. Joe Reston was an older guy I met a few years ago, and we hit it off."

"You actually settled down with someone older than you?" Michelle asked, her voice cold. "I remember when you used to hit on the boys I brought home from school, before I knew better."

Joan smiled a little at that and snickered, but continued without otherwise acknowledging Michelle's comment.

"Joe wanted to retire in Florida, and I thought that sounded fine. We moved down there, and we had a great time together, for a while."

"What happened? He got tired of your shit?" Michelle asked.

"He died."

Michelle almost felt bad about her comment.

"I'm sorry for him," she replied. "When was this?"

"About four months ago, just before Christmas. I had hoped I might be able to continue collecting his Social Security checks, you know, as his common-law wife." She sighed disgustedly. "Turns out Florida abolished common-law marriage something like fifty years ago. And we were only together for six years, so apparently, it wouldn't have counted as common-law marriage anyway." She scoffed and shook her head, and it occurred to Michelle that she didn't seem very broken up about his death just a few months before.

"He did leave me a little," Joan continued, "but barely enough to make it worth the trouble."

"Worth what trouble?"

"Sticking around for the funeral, all the legal bullshit, you know, sitting with the family at the lawyer's office for the reading of the will, and the inevitable relatives who are pissed that he didn't leave more to them."

Michelle wondered if her face was accurately showing how disgusted she was.

"Anyway, I decided to come back home. I figured I'd been away long enough."

"So, if you didn't get Bill's money," Michelle said, feeling her energy flagging, "what are you living on now?"

"Like I said, I did get some. But I got a job, too" Joan shrugged. "I got a decent recommendation from the last nursing home I worked for here. It wasn't too hard." She snorted. "I do miss being retired, though. That was sweet while it lasted." She pulled a flask out of the purse sitting on the chair beside her and took a swallow. "Anyway, here I am."

"Well, you can go now," Michelle said, closing her eyes and sighing heavily.

"Not on your life, baby girl. I'm your mama. I'm going to take care of you."

Michelle opened her eyes again and looked at Joan.

"I don't need you to take care of me," she said.

"Well, honey, you know that's a load of bullshit. According to the doctor, you're in stage three of your HIV infection. You're in full-blown AIDS now, sweetie. It's only downhill from here."

"Fuck," Michelle said as, exhausted, she drifted off into an uneasy sleep.

31

Suzy's face was scrunched up as she opened her eyes, trying to reconcile the cold and brutal Joan she had just witnessed in the episode with the sweet, emotional, heartbroken one she had met and visited with. It was as if they were two different people.

Then, she remembered the earlier differences she had noticed between Michelle's memories and her own, and wondered how much of this version of Joan was colored by Michelle's prejudices and the lifelong hatred she had cultivated toward her mother. Then again, we always try to put on a better face when meeting someone new. Joan was likely no exception. Perhaps the true version of Joan was somewhere in between the two versions that Suzy had experienced.

Once again, she felt the uneasy sensation of being watched, but after taking a glance out the window – and not seeing anyone – she decided to chalk it up to Michelle's feelings bleeding through from the episodes into Suzy's consciousness. Although she realized that she hadn't noticed Michelle feeling that paranoid sensation for a few episodes now.

That led to the thought that perhaps it was more than just her feelings. What if Michelle's psychological issues were transmitting to Suzy, as well? Would Suzy come out of this actually experiencing Michelle's addictions, and having to go through withdrawal?

Of course, maybe someone really was watching Suzy, plotting some kind of nefarious machination against her, and Suzy, being inexperienced with such things, just wasn't able to actually spot them. But she couldn't figure out why anyone would be doing such a thing.

Suzy wasn't sure if either alternative was better than the other.

A third alternative came to her mind when she felt Michelle's presence, and realized that her spirit was likely watching her.

§

Michelle wasn't entirely sure how it happened, but she had her suspicions.

She sighed, lying in the new hospital-style bed that was now standing in her living room. The wing-back chair had been pushed to the side to make room for it beside the window. It was nice that she was able to be in her own home, looking out the window at her neighborhood. Then, she turned her head slightly – she had energy for little more than that – and saw her mother sitting on the sofa reading a magazine. She rolled her eyes with disgust and looked back out the window.

Michelle had been stunned, completely dismayed, when Dr. Conrad suggested that she go into hospice care.

"B-but," she had stammered, "that's for someone who's close to death, isn't it?" She recalled the look on his grandfatherly face, his eyebrows raised, as he looked over his glasses at her.

"Honey," he said softly, "remember I told you that your systems are shutting down? I'm afraid your body can't fight it off anymore."

Michelle looked at him, her face gradually reflecting the seriousness of what he was saying.

"You're telling me that I'm going to be dead soon?"

"I can't say for sure when," he replied sympathetically, tilting his head, "but I'm afraid it's coming. We can do some things to delay it a little, or at least to make you a little more comfortable, but yes, I'm afraid the end is approaching."

Michelle felt her eyes fill with tears, only partly from the news itself. Mostly, it was from the genuine sympathy Dr. Conrad was directing toward her. She never even saw that from her own mother.

She asked for time to think about it, to which he nodded and said, "Of course."

The next thing she knew, the arrangements were made, and her mother was in charge.

There's no fucking way she would have granted her mother power of attorney over her affairs. She sure as hell didn't want her to be the last person she ever saw. But, that's the way it worked out, and she had a feeling she knew how.

A number of past occasions came to her mind. One memory in particular came in sharp detail. One cold January when she was twelve, Michelle had gotten sick with a really bad sore throat. Her mother made her drink lots of water, but after two or three days, her symptoms weren't getting any better. After doing a brief examination of her, Joan determined that she had strep throat.

Michelle remembered having mixed feelings about going to the doctor, but she knew that starting a prescription would likely help her kick the infection. Her mother, though, didn't want to take her to the doctor. Though Michelle knew that Joan had decent health coverage through her job at the nursing home, in order to keep the premiums lower, she had opted for a higher deductible. Seeing as how it was the beginning of the year, she was starting over on the deductible and didn't want to pay for an office visit.

Besides, she insisted that, with her medical training and her experience with medications, she knew what Michelle needed just as well as any doctor would.

Instead, she took a prescription slip from one of a few pads she had swiped and stored in a drawer in their apartment, and she sorted through a few doctor's signatures that she had traced and saved. In a couple of minutes, she had forged a prescription for an antibiotic. She chose a drug that she knew had a generic version and saved herself some more bucks.

Michelle now suspected that her mother had done some more of her creative paperwork. The day before she was to be discharged, a man and woman from the hospice service showed up. Joan produced a few sheets of paper to show them and Michelle tried to snatch them out of her hand. Her motor control was deteriorating, though, and she crumpled the papers. One of them, she saw, was the application for in-home hospice care. The other was a document granting power of attorney to Joan.

Both had Michelle's signature on them.

"I didn't sign these," she insisted, but her words were garbled. She tried saying it again, but again, even to her own ears, she sounded as if she was drunk.

She tried to hold the papers up to show the hospice people, to explain that they were forgeries, but her hands went wild, and the woman stepped back to avoid being hit by her. Tears came to Michelle's eyes as she tried to explain the situation, but all that came out was gibberish.

"Baby girl," Joan said, her face dripping with sympathy for the benefit of the hospice representatives, "you need to leave this to me, as you directed." She took the papers from Michelle's hands and smoothed them out. Michelle didn't have the strength to put up a fight.

The weakness and garbled speech were troubling, though. Just yesterday, she had experienced something similar, but to a lesser degree. At first, she was afraid that the disease was progressing even faster than expected.

As it turned out, she had accidentally pressed the button for the PCA pump to inject a dose of morphine when it wasn't needed. After that, she moved the handset to the table beside her bed rather than allowing it to rest by her hand.

Michelle turned and looked at the handset on the table, beside where her mother was standing, trying to determine if it was still in exactly the same position as when she last placed it there. To her chagrin, she couldn't remember. She felt so tired, her brain so foggy.

She lay her head back and watched her mother, feeling her heart pumping frantically in her chest, the suspicion smoldering inside her, but impotent to do or say anything.

As the drug that she was certain was there continued its effects, Michelle had finally given in and fell asleep.

The following day, she was discharged into her mother's care. When her mind was clear, she had tried, several times, to explain to nurses or orderlies that the documents her mother had were *not valid. Given the fact that mental deterioration and memory issues were symptoms to be expected, though, her complaints fell on deaf ears. The best she received was a sympathetic nod and a pat on the arm.*

32

She was already there, doing her thing, whatever that was, when he arrived early in the morning. He parked two houses down, in the same spot where he had spent a good portion of yesterday, and he could already see her sitting in that chair by the window. This early, the window was dappled with reflections from the neighborhood and the pastel sunrise, but once he had picked her out, he could see her form through them.

He had made it a point to get there early, just in case there might be a way to get close and overhear any exchange between the two women. He was surprised that it wasn't early enough. Or maybe the younger woman had spent the night. She was slumped over in the chair when he arrived, as if she was asleep.

He shook his head, his forehead crinkled, his eyebrows puckered together. What could possibly possess this person to sit there all day long, perfectly still, with only an occasional break to get up and stretch and move around? He chuckled when he realized that he was doing exactly the same thing.

But it was because of her. It was her fault that he was sitting on his ass in his hot car all day long.

She took an early drive out to Marblehead, to that castle, and once or twice, it looked as if she might have spotted him again. Driving into the sun, it was harder to keep her in sight from farther back, but he had hoped that having the sun in her eyes would make it harder for her to see him, as well.

But it looked as if, a couple of times she was focusing closely on her rear-view mirror, and once almost sideswiped another car in the process, so he decided to back off. By this time, having followed her yesterday, he figured he knew where she was going, so he kept more cars between them.

The only thing he learned from that trip was that she had a little dog. She had a conversation with a neighbor, but he hadn't been able to get close enough to hear any of what they talked about.

So now, here he was parked back in Saugus. At least he had thought to bring a book with him today, and a large Thermos jug of cold water. Could be worse, he thought, as he filled up the tall plastic tumbler standing in the cup holder. Outside, it was still cool and comfortable. The temperature would rise as the day went on, but for now, it wasn't so bad.

He picked up the book, *Trainspotting*, and delved back into the escapades of Mark Renton and his crew, glancing up toward the house occasionally.

33

She didn't want to engage her mother in conversation. She despised this woman more than anybody she had ever known. Michelle found herself hoping that she would die soon, except that there were still things she needed to do.

She just didn't know how she could do them.

If only she could call Amy, or Sheree. Or even Suzy Drummond. No, she corrected herself, Suzy Quinn. She had heard about Mark's death a few years ago, and she had spent a few days crying about that. She knew of Suzy's recently discovered abilities, and about how she had occasionally used these abilities to help others. A self-sacrificing person like that would probably be willing to help her out.

But she didn't know how much Mark had told her about their relationship. Did he tell her what a mess she was? Suzy could very likely tell her to take a flying fuck.

It didn't matter, though. It was a moot point. She couldn't call anyone. Her mother kept her phone and, in fact, had canceled her account.

Joan had raved about the house, even before Michelle had been discharged. Having made the arrangements for home hospice, Joan had fallen in love with the place. Though it was small, having seen where she lived before, Michelle could understand why. It was still larger than the apartment that she and Mark had visited, with more architectural interest and more stylish décor than Joan ever had.

Knowing there was no mortgage likely made it that much more attractive. Michelle cringed imagining the way it will likely end up after a few months of her mother living here.

If only she could get to her safety deposit box, where she had placed her will. She hadn't actually retained a lawyer to draw it up for her. To be honest, she didn't think her trivial "estate" warranted that kind of expense. But she had created the will based on a template she had found online, then had it notarized when she signed it.

But again, there was no way she could get to the bank, no way she could call anyone she could trust to help her with it. Angela, the hospice nurse, would be there soon for her daily visit, and Michelle had a feeling she would take her seriously. But Joan always made it a point to stay right there when Angela was around. There could be no privacy, no confidential talk, no request for help. Any negative comment or plea for help would be explained away by the disease.

She was trapped.

She looked out at the sunny July day. It was her neighborhood, her home, but she was so detached from all of it now.

Joan had placed a few magazines on the bed within Michelle's reach, but she didn't have the mental stamina to even skim through them. That's not to say her brain wasn't working. She had been doing a lot of thinking as she lay there. Some of the things her mother had said, and the way she acted, had been rattling around in Michelle's head.

She didn't know if the conclusions she was forming, assumptions really, were accurate or not. They could just as likely be a result of her deteriorating brain functions, or drug-induced hallucinations.

At this point, though, she decided she had nothing more to lose.

"So," she said, hearing the fatigue weighing her voice down, "how did Joe die?"

Joan looked up at Michelle from her magazine, her eyebrows puckered.

"What?"

"Joe Reston, how did he die?"

"Heart attack. Why?"

"I don't know. Just wondering if there were any warning signs."

"He had high blood pressure. He was on medication for it, but I guess he forgot to take it. Kind of like you and your AIDS medication."

"Hmm."

"Why this sudden interest in Joe?"

"You just didn't seem that broken up about it for someone who had been with him for six years, and since it just happened four months ago."

"What are you getting at, baby girl?" Joan asked, her tone getting a little harder. She laid the magazine down on the sofa, giving Michelle her full attention.

"I just remember how well you know drugs."

"Yeah," Joan smirked, "I guess you're pretty familiar with them, yourself."

"Only one or two. But you knew exactly what drug I needed whenever I got sick. And you were usually pretty fucking shifty in the way you got them."

Joan looked at Michelle for a few moments, then her mouth curved slightly into a tight smile.

"Very good," she nodded, her face wearing an expression that almost looked like admiration. "Except with Joe, it didn't require prescription drugs. All it took was sneaking some ibuprofen to interfere with his blood pressure meds.

"Now Paul Hoffmeister, he took a little more creativity. You know how tough it is to make someone who's perfectly healthy to drop dead of natural causes? I mean he was eighty years old, but he could easily have gone on another ten or fifteen.

"But I managed to live for a couple of years on what he left me. Not that it was very much." She snorted. "You've seen how I live."

Michelle was horrified that her assumption about Joe had been correct, and worse, that he wasn't the first. The fatigue and the pain in all of her joints, though, made her seem more calm and composed about the information than she really felt.

"I'm impressed," Joan said. "You've got a better head on your shoulders than I ever gave you credit for."

Michelle looked at Joan, her lifelong loathing now mixed with revulsion at how much of a monster she turned out to be.

"I'm curious why you're admitting it all to me," Michelle said. Joan shrugged and gestured toward Michelle's weakened and shrunken body.

"What are you going to do? It's not like you're going to be around to call the cops on me."

"That's true." Michelle took a deep breath and heaved a heavy sigh. "I could tell Angela, though."

Joan chuckled and shook her head, her face wearing an expression that said, 'you poor, stupid child.'

"Honey, all I gotta do is press that button and send another bolus or two of morphine into your veins, and you'll either be a blathering idiot, or you'll be out cold."

"Sure," Michelle agreed. "But while morphine starts working on the pain right away, it takes five or ten minutes for that full effect you're talking about."

"So?"

"So, Angela just drove up." Joan bolted up from the sofa and looked out the window. The nurse's car was parked at the curb, and Angela was gathering things up from the seat. She would be at the door in a minute or less.

In a panic, Joan looked frantically around, trying to decide what to do. She grabbed the drape and jerked it partly closed, while Michelle looked on with an amused smile on her face, the first one she had worn in a while.

Joan looked around again and was visibly trying to calm herself and think clearly. She grabbed a throw pillow from the sofa and turned back toward Michelle. In a moment, Michelle could see what she was thinking, and the amused smile faded. Joan hesitated only a second or two, then pressed the pillow down over Michelle's face.

Despite her desire to die a few minutes earlier, Michelle's survival instinct kicked in, and she tried to fight her off, but her feeble body was no match for Joan's. She felt the pressure of the rough pillow against her face as she struggled in vain to draw air into her lungs. She felt a tightening in her chest, and a moment of panic as it felt like her lungs were going to explode.

Another couple of seconds and the blackness that she saw seeped into her consciousness, and Michelle could feel her other senses fading, until all was dark and silent.

§

Suzy came out of the episode, but oddly enough, it was as if she was still seeing the final moments of Michelle's life. She was aware of her surroundings, though, and she realized that the pillow that had smothered the life out of Michelle was being held against her own face.

As her own panic took over, she tried to push the pillow away, but she couldn't get good leverage. She clawed at the hands holding the pillow, feeling her nails dig in, and she could feel sticky blood on them, but the hands held tight.

Feeling her own life slipping away, she heard screaming, but she couldn't tell if it was her own.

34

He looked up from his book and frowned when he saw the car pull up, and he instinctively slouched down in his seat. He didn't expect to see her return this morning. But then, she didn't come back last night, which he thought was unusual. He thought he knew her pattern – leaving for work around 7:30 a.m., coming back around 5:30 p.m. But he hadn't been watching that long. Perhaps there was some variation that he wasn't aware of yet.

Something about her caught his attention, though, and he put the book down on the seat beside him. She shut off her car and just sat there, looking up toward the house. With the current angle of the sun, there were fewer reflections, and it was a little easier to see in the front window of the house. The younger woman was still in her place in the wing-back chair.

Apparently satisfied – about what, he couldn't imagine – the other woman opened the door and got out of her car. But she was moving stealthily. She kept looking around as if she didn't want to be seen. Slouched down as he was behind the dashboard, he knew she couldn't see him if he remained perfectly still.

She quietly opened the front door and slipped inside. A few seconds later, he saw her in the front window, and she pulled the drapes closed. The other woman hadn't moved a muscle.

Something strange was going on, stranger than what he had already observed, and he decided that it required investigation.

He got out of his car and crossed the street, making sure to stay hidden behind the large trunk of the old maple tree next door, just in case she came back out or opened the drapes again, but trying not to look as suspicious as the woman did before him. When he got up against the trunk of the maple, he peeked around it, then made a dash toward the front porch.

He tried the doorknob, and it was unlocked. Leaning hard against it, he pushed the door open, and his senses were suddenly assaulted by the bizarre scene taking place in the little living room.

Ripped from his hands, the door slammed, seemingly of its own volition, and it suddenly felt as if the air pressure had increased tenfold. It was difficult to pull air into his lungs as the atmosphere pressed heavily against his body. With the drapes only partly closed, it was darker than he expected it to be, while the temperature in the room felt frigid. There was a low-frequency sound, a deep hum that filled his ears and vibrated his gut, and he felt as if he was going to vomit.

There in the living room, the older woman was pressing a pillow over the face of the younger woman in the chair, while the younger woman struggled to disengage her would-be killer. As intense as that was, that wasn't what really captured his attention. A hideous, demonic-looking figure that reminded him of the angel of death in *Raiders of the Lost Ark* was circling around them, shimmering like the embers of a fire on the verge of being rekindled.

The wraith was gesticulating frantically, trying to push against the older woman and screaming, "Mother! Mother, stop!" He had the fleeting thought that that was a weird thing for the demon to say. Though the figure's gesticulations were directed at the woman herself, the apparition's hand kept passing right through the woman as if she wasn't even there.

The woman kept glancing up at this figure circling her and, judging by the look on her face, was apparently terror-stricken by the sight of it. Still, though, she tried to remain focused on her goal.

Her goal of killing the younger woman.

She kept one hand pressing down the pillow on the young woman's face, leaning the weight of her body over it, while trying, futilely, to bat the angel of death away.

Despite the intensity of the scene before him, he realized that the younger woman was struggling less. Her life seemed to be ebbing away, and he knew he needed to do something. Working against the strain of breathing, he managed to pull a deep breath into his lungs.

"Mother!" he shouted and, despite the pressure bearing against him from all sides, he rushed forward, grabbing her arm and yanking her off the other woman. He snatched the pillow off the young woman's face.

The terror in Joan's eyes faded slightly as she looked at him.

"Nicky?" she said.

Ignoring her, and the angel of death, he turned his attention to the woman in the wing-back chair. She wasn't dead. She was gasping for breath, though, her hands grasping her chest, as she sucked deep, raspy breaths into her starved lungs.

Seeing that she was apparently okay, he looked back up toward his other major concern, the angel of death, only to find that it had changed its appearance. The terrifying demonic wraith he had seen earlier now stood in front of him, looking at him in shock.

And it looked like his sister.

"Michelle?" he said. He was struggling for breath himself now, not only from the atmosphere, but from emotion, as he looked at the image of his dead sister.

"Nicky," she said, her voice cracking with feeling.

Nicky stared at her, his mouth hanging open, and he felt tears coming to his eyes.

"I didn't think I'd ever see you again," he whispered.

He didn't notice Joan trying to make a getaway, but Michelle did, and in a blurry blink of an eye, she flew to

187

the front door, slamming it closed as Joan fumbled with the doorknob. Michelle looked down at her hand as if surprised that she had finally been able to have an effect on something solid.

With Michelle's apparition less agitated and frantic, the room was beginning to feel a little more normal, the air a little more breathable. Hearing electronic beeps behind him, Nicky turned and saw the younger woman, her breathing becoming more normal now, putting her cell phone to her ear.

"Yes," she panted into the phone, "I'd like to report an attempted murder, and at least three other murders." Her eyes were throwing daggers at Joan.

"You little bitch," Joan hissed, coming back around the sofa.

"No, I'm not in danger anymore," Suzy continued, ignoring Joan as she gave the address to the 911 dispatcher. After a few seconds, Suzy slipped her phone back into her purse.

"I never should have called you," Joan continued. "I thought you might actually do something useful, like getting rid of ghosts."

"Yes, Mother," Michelle replied, her otherworldly voice dripping with sarcasm, "I insisted you call her so she could get rid of me." Nicky noticed that Michelle's appearance changed to resemble that angel of death again when she spat out her response to Joan. "But then, you already did that, didn't you?"

Suzy slowly, unsteadily, pushed herself up out of the chair, testing her muscles as she felt life seeping back into her body.

"Shut up and sit down," she said coldly, pointing to the love seat.

"Who's gonna make me?" Joan asked like a belligerent juvenile, but she immediately turned her head as she sensed movement, and she saw Michelle's grinning death mask next to her. "Get away from me, you fucking little whore!" Looking into the cold eyes of the ghost, her voice quivered, and lacked the conviction she seemed to want to convey, but she didn't back down.

"You and your little asshole brother were always such a pain in my ass." She started waving her arms for emphasis, which seemed to increase her boldness. "God, I was so fucking glad when I was finally rid of the both of you. You were nothing but a fucking nuisance."

"Button it up, Beulah!" Suzy said. Joan hadn't noticed her approaching, but she suddenly felt two cold bits of metal touch her side. She heard a loud crackling sound and felt the electric shock as the stun gun sent 30,000 volts through her body, and she collapsed on the love seat.

"Oh my god," Suzy said, looking at Michelle and Nicky, how did you put up with that for so long?"

§

The EMT had determined that Suzy was fit, since Nicky had come on the scene in the nick of time. The police had taken Suzy's statement and hauled Joan away in handcuffs, cursing and insisting on her innocence the whole way. They seemed a little suspicious concerning Suzy's accusation of Joan's murder of Michelle, Joe Reston and Paul Hoffmeister. But they promised that they would look into the cases, and any other dubious deaths connected to Joan Rossi.

When the last cop finally left, Suzy collapsed back into the wing-back chair and heaved a heavy sigh. Nicky sat down on the sofa with a similar reaction.

Michelle, who had remained hidden from the police and the EMTs, effervesced into visibility before Suzy and Nicky now.

The police had opened the drapes to provide more light for the EMTs. Suzy pulled them closed again after they left to discourage the prying eyes of neighbors. In the dimmer light, Michelle's apparition shimmered like the embers of a fire.

"Thank you," she said to Suzy.

"Michelle," Suzy said, her voice little more than a breath with tone, "oh my god." Tears filled her eyes as she looked at her and she recalled memories of the times she had dismissed Michelle as simply an inconsequential loser. "I wish so badly I had been there for you."

Nicky was not quite as restrained. He broke down in tears when he saw Michelle standing in front of him again, lifelike and vital.

"So many times," he said between sobs, "I wanted to come here and see you. But I was ashamed. I was such a huge fuck-up."

"Nicky," Michelle effused, shaking her head, "honey, you have no idea. You couldn't have been a bigger fuck-up than me."

"Oh yeah?" he said, getting his sobs a little more under control. With an effort, he took a deep breath and let it out slowly. "I did two stretches at Cedar Junction. It wasn't until the second one, for breaking and entering and larceny, to get money for drugs, that I finally realized how fucked up I really was."

He rubbed the tears out of his eyes and wiped them on his shorts.

"I resolved that I wasn't going back. So, I started a twelve-step program there in prison, and I kept at it ever since I got out. It was that eighth step that finally got me over here again."

Michelle nodded, sadly remembering those steps herself.

"You did better than me," Michelle said. "I hardly even bothered with the steps."

Nicky's eyes, continuously glossed over with tears, scarcely strayed from Michelle's apparition.

"I knew I had to make amends to you, for taking advantage of you, for using you as my supplier. I only came around when I needed more shit. But I was so ashamed of what I'd been like. It took me nearly a month to work up the courage to get myself over here.

"And when I finally did, just a little over a week ago," he stopped, pausing as he tried to keep his emotions under control, "they were carrying you out in a body bag."

The tears threatened again, but he took a deep breath and held them in check.

"Mother was here, the fucking bitch," he continued, his voice cold and hard now, "trying to act all broken up about it. But I noticed when whoever she was talking to looked away, the emotion vanished from her face.

"I started coming by, just to see what she was doing. She settled right in like she fucking owned the place."

"Unfortunately," Michelle said, "she does. She forged a bunch of documents, including a power of attorney form. She signed everything over to herself. Not that I had that much, but I guess the house is hers now."

"I'm sure there are experts who'll be able to tell that they're forgeries," Suzy said.

"I hope so," Michelle replied.

"When you started coming around," Nicky continued to Suzy, "I started watching you, too, and I'd see you sitting in that chair all day. I couldn't figure out what you were doing here. I'm sorry if I scared you."

"Yeah, you did," Suzy said with a smile and a roll of her eyes. "But I understand." Then, she frowned and looked at him. "Are you a detective, or what? I mean, how could you spend all day sitting out there watching me?"

"For now, I'm just driving for DoorDash," he shrugged. "I can pretty much make my own hours. The last few days, I haven't made much."

Suzy nodded, then, after a moment she turned back to Michelle.

"I understand why you stayed around," she said, "to try to bring your mother to justice. But why show me all of those episodes with Mark?"

Michelle seemed hesitant to look at Suzy, sadness showing in her eyes.

"I admit part of it may have just been vanity." She smiled and looked off into the distance. "I felt good about myself when I was with him. And I actually got myself clean for a while, with his help." She shook her head. "But there was more to it than that. I wanted you to see how he dealt with me, and how he felt about you. And how he helped me keep my house."

She directed her gaze pointedly at Suzy.

"And I want you to take my safety deposit box key."

"Yes," Suzy replied, "I remember you thinking about that in the last episode."

"I made a will and put it there. Because of Mark paying off my house, I willed it to him. But," she paused, her voice becoming quieter, "since he died, I guess it will go to you, now."

"Michelle," Suzy said, "that's so sweet and thoughtful of you. I mean that sincerely. But I don't need your house. It's a lovely home, really. But I'm very happy where I am." She looked at Nicky. "Besides, I think it should go to your next of kin."

Nicky looked up at Suzy, surprise on his face.

"Oh, Suzy," Michelle said, "I wish I could have been as good a person as you are."

"Oh stop," Suzy replied, "I'm plenty fucked up myself."

§

By early afternoon, Michelle's face wore an expression that looked like contentment, that seemed to express that she was done, settled. Nicky seemed to recognize what that meant.

"I just got you back, sort of," he said. "I don't want you to go."

Michelle smiled sadly.

"I know, Nicky, but I think I need to." She looked over at Suzy for confirmation. Suzy shook her head and shrugged, implying that it wasn't her decision. Michelle thought for a moment and nodded. "Yeah, I need to 'move on,' as you called it." Then, she shrugged, herself. "So, how do I do that?"

Suzy remembered when she stood on that very precipice herself a couple of years before, when trying to save Fin from the ghost that left him comatose.

"You should be able to see the hint of a door, a bright white outline."

"Yeah," Michelle replied, casting a disparaging glance over her left shoulder, "the fucking thing's been following me around."

Suzy smiled.

"Instead of trying to ignore it, when you actually turn your attention to it, it should open." Suzy shrugged again. "When you're ready, you just go through it."

"I really don't want you to go," Nicky said again, his eyes glossing over. "I'm going to miss you so much."

"I know, Nicky," Michelle replied. "I'll miss you, too. But I think I need to do this." She held her hands out and looked at her flickering apparition. "I can't exactly stay around like this."

"I wish I'd been a better brother," Nicky said.

"I wish I'd been a better sister," Michelle replied.

Suzy shook her head and joined in, remembering the remorse she expressed when she first saw Michelle.

"I wish I'd been a better friend," she said.

"Looks like we've all got regrets," Michelle said. Then, she glanced over her left shoulder again. "Maybe that's what that door's for. We can get rid of our regrets and start fresh."

"I hope so," Suzy said.

"I love you, sis," Nicky said, the tears making their way down his cheeks now.

"I love you, too." Michelle smiled. "But I feel a whole lot better about leaving you now. Keep up the good work."

Nicky nodded, sniffing as he wiped the tears away, only to be replaced by more. Michelle looked at Suzy.

"Wish me luck," she said.

"You don't need luck," Suzy replied. "I think you're going to be just fine."

The three of them exchanged tearful looks and smiles. Then, before she got too emotional, Michelle vanished in a bright flash of light.

35

Bobbing boats were scattered across the harbor, attached to their mooring buoys. It was a beautiful July afternoon, and a lot of boats had been taken out, their assigned buoys waiting empty in the harbor for them to return.

Suzy stood looking out over the harbor from Terri's house. Terri had told her to go on out while she set her dinner cooking. Suzy was concerned that she was keeping Terri from something she needed to do, but Terri assured her that it was just a casserole and it had to bake for a while.

After Suzy said goodbye to Nicky, she made the drive back home to Marblehead. She cuddled with Ursula for a while, giving the dog some much-needed affection, while hoping to calm her own fears and anxiety.

So far, it hadn't worked.

She was concerned about the fact that just after she accepted Fin's marriage proposal, she began these episodes with Mark in them. And once she started them, she craved them, came back again and again. She couldn't get enough, even though he had been dead for almost five years now.

It didn't bode well for their future marital bliss that she was still so attached to her dead husband.

"Ready?"

Suzy jumped, having been so deeply inside her own head that she hadn't heard Terri approach.

"Yeah," Suzy nodded nervously as they started walking down toward the dock.

"You don't have to do this, you know," Terri said, noticing her tension. "We all have unfinished business." Suzy looked at her, thinking about Michelle. "God will make us whole again if we just give ourselves to Him."

The words irritated Suzy, the concept kind of grating against her. But she reminded herself that Terri was just trying to help.

"Thanks," she replied, "but I think I do need to do this. It's not just about Mark and Emma, although that's a big part of it. But I haven't been on a boat since it happened, and living out here, that's almost unheard of." She looked at Terri again, and Terri nodded. Then, Suzy patted her purse. "Besides, I have these thirteen rats that I need to offer up to Beelzebub at the accident site."

Terri looked at her without saying a word. She shook her head, but Suzy was pretty sure she was trying not to smile.

They climbed aboard the 28-foot cruiser – *Art's DioSeas* – and disconnected the fore and aft lines. Settling into the seats, Terri started it up. She backed away from the dock and began slowly working her way between the boats and buoys in the harbor.

"*Art's DioSeas*?" Suzy inquired.

"My husband's name is Art," Terri replied.

"Ah," Suzy nodded.

The farther they got from shore, the more nervous Suzy felt. Being out on the water again, her heart was hammering in her chest, and as they moved northward, she looked up toward her house, imagining Ursula curled up in there. The thought calmed her a little, though she wished she was up there with her.

"You know," Terri said with a smile, "I was so glad to hear you talking about getting yourself right with the Lord. That'll go a long ways toward getting you installed at His right hand."

"Terri," Suzy said, feeling that little bit of calm get tossed overboard, "I'm sorry, but I'm afraid I have a confession." She looked at Terri, willing herself to continue. "I'm afraid I misled you just a bit."

"What do you mean?" Terri asked.

Suzy sighed.

"Terri, I'm not what you or anyone else would consider a Christian."

"I don't understand." Terri looked askance at Suzy as she steered the boat, her eyebrows knitted together. "Why did you say what you did?"

"Because I'm a jerk. I needed to come out here on the harbor and you have a boat." She looked at Terri and shook her head. "I'm not even sure I believe in heaven and hell. But if there is a hell, that's probably where I'll be heading after this."

"How–" Terri scoffed, "how can you not believe in Heaven and Hell? If there's no Heaven or Hell, then what incentive is there to be good?"

"Have you seen how screwed up the world is?" Suzy asked. "You really think that belief is saving us?"

"It helps. Just think of the absolute anarchy that would exist if nobody believed."

"Most people, regardless of whether they're Christians or atheists, have a built-in sense of right and wrong. It has nothing to do with that Judeo-Christian belief in a heaven and hell."

Terri raised her eyebrows when she looked at Suzy.

"I think you're underselling the incentive that the Lord has given us."

"Well, I've got news for you, Terri. Anybody who needs a promise of a reward or a threat of punishment as an incentive to be a good person isn't a good person. He's just a selfish asshole."

As they maneuvered past the last of the boats, even with the Marblehead Light, Terri looked at Suzy again, a stern look on her face. She shut down the engine and they bobbed on the waves.

"So, I suppose you have some kind of pagan ritual you want to perform out here? Are you hoping to contact the ghost of your dead husband?"

Suzy sighed.

"Realistically, no. I mean, to be absolutely honest with you, yes, the hope is there. But I don't expect it."

Terri was still looking at Suzy, trying to decide whether to continue. Suzy sighed.

"Terri, I'm not going to conjure up the soul of my dead husband and daughter. I'm not going to drag you down to hell with me. And I don't have thirteen rats in my purse to sacrifice to Beelzebub. Seriously, this is just for closure."

"Where?" Terri asked, her tone miffed.

"Over there," Suzy pointed to the left, "just below the fort."

Terri looked at Suzy for a few moments, then started the boat. Turning to port, she headed across the harbor toward where Fort Sewall sat hunched on a northeastern point of mainland Marblehead.

The closer they got, the more anxious Suzy became. The day couldn't have been more different. The accident was on a cold and grey October, and today was a warm, bright and sunny July day. Still, just seeing the rocks drawing near sent a chill down her spine.

And what if Mark *was* here? What if Suzy *was* able to make contact with him? Would that solve anything? What good would it do? Would she throw herself in the harbor to be with him forever?

She knew she wouldn't, but she didn't know what it would mean for Fin and their intended nuptials. Could she really pledge herself to Fin knowing that Mark was out here on the harbor? Would she convince him to move on? Would he do it?

She shivered, and it helped to bring her back to reality. She looked at Terri and pointed to starboard, a little more to the north. Terri turned the wheel and Suzy tensed, picturing the overturned rowboat that they had struck. But the water was clear today.

"This is fine," she said. Terri got up and went to the anchor control. She pressed a button, dropping the anchor.

Once she felt it catch, she tied it off and shut down the engine.

As Terri sat back down, Suzy stood up. Trying not to hyperventilate, she grasped the gunwale tightly with both hands, peering over the side. In the bright sunshine, the water was a brilliant greenish-blue. She closed her eyes, opening her mind and her heart as she did when trying to enter an episode.

She thought about Mark, her own abundant memories of him, as well as the new ones she had just acquired from Michelle. She pictured Mark and Emma on that last day, sitting side-by-side at the back of the boat as Suzy steered. She remembered the very last image she ever saw of them when she turned and looked back. Mark smiled at her, squinting into the cold wind. Emma laughed, a bright, sparkling sound barely heard over the sound of the boat's motor, and the wind and the waves slapping against the hull as the wind blew their hair.

Just after that, she turned back toward the front and saw the overturned rowboat, their cruiser glancing off the barely submerged hull. Her too-late efforts to avoid it sent them onto the rocks below Fort Sewall, which she also frantically tried to avoid, unsuccessfully.

Sometime between that last look and hearing the crack of their hull against the rock, Mark and Emma had gone overboard. Divers couldn't retrieve their bodies until the next day.

Suzy stood at the side of Terri's boat, her consciousness as open as she could possibly manage, welcoming Mark and Emma. She uttered an apology, a meager offering, she thought, considering what she was apologizing for, but it was heartfelt and sincere.

She opened her eyes, feeling a little surprised to not see Mark in front of her. He had felt so real the last couple of days from her episodes of Michelle. Her own thoughts and memories had been so vivid.

She didn't know how much time had passed, but she was finally convinced that there was nothing here. Mark and Emma weren't waiting here for her, to show her that they were fine.

They were gone.

Suzy loosened her grip on the gunwale and slowly backed away, dropping back into her seat, while Terri watched quietly, even respectfully.

There *was* something, though. Suzy's heart wasn't pounding any longer. She was calm as she sat there, rocking with the waves. And even more than any physical manifestation, she felt an inner peace that she hadn't felt in a long time.

Fin's laid-back nature calmed her, but even when she had been in his presence, she realized that there had always been a lack, an emptiness hovering somewhere in the background. Perhaps this was something felt by everyone who experienced an unfinished marriage or an abridged motherhood.

Now, that emptiness was, perhaps not gone, but not so acute. She looked back out at the water and wondered if, somehow, it was Mark, or was it she herself who had done the forgiving?

Whatever it was, she felt free. Mark was her past. Fin was her present, and her future.

Suzy sighed and turned to Terri.

"That's it?" Terri asked.

Suzy smiled and nodded.

"Ready to go back now?"

Suzy nodded again, her body feeling completely relaxed.

"Well, I guess that wasn't *too* bad," Terri said. She started up the boat and moved it forward a bit. She started the windlass, pulling up the line. Once the anchor was up and locked, she turned the boat toward home.

The trip back was quiet as she allowed Suzy space to process her experience. As she finally eased the boat up against the dock, Suzy was more in the present. She got up and tied off the aft line while Terri did the fore line.

They climbed out of the boat onto the dock, and Terri looked at Suzy.

"So," Terri said, "did you get what you went out there for?"

"Yeah, I think so."

"You're a strange one, Suzy Quinn," she said. Suzy smiled at her. "But I like you."

"Really?" Suzy said, her face scrunched up in self-deprecating disdain. "Why?"

Terri smiled and shook her head.

"I guess if we're going to be friends, we'll just have to agree to disagree on some things."

"You mean like my being a smartass?" Suzy asked.

"Nah," Terri replied. "Nothing wrong with being a smartass, as long as you don't blaspheme or take the Lord's name in vain."

Suzy almost said, "Well, Jesus Christ, there's no god-damn way I'd ever do that." But, fortunately, her inner filters engaged in time.

36

"There's my little bear," came a voice from the front door. The jingling of Ursula's tags told Suzy that the dog was receiving vigorous pets and scratches from Fin. Suzy smiled and put her cup of tea down, standing up from her place on the sofa.

"And there's my near missus," Fin said, leaving Ursula wiggling at his feet when he saw Suzy coming to greet him.

"Near misses?" Suzy echoed, frowning at him, but molding herself into his embrace.

"Near Missus MacKinley," Fin smiled. "As in 'almost Missus MacKinley.' Or Ms. Quinn," he corrected. "Sorry, I forgot." Suzy looked up at him, confusion etched onto her face. "Okay," Fin conceded, "I guess that might be a pun that only really works in writing."

"It's still good to have you back, goofball," Suzy said, "even your silly wordplay."

"It's good to be back," Fin replied, gazing deeply into Suzy's eyes before going in for a deep kiss.

"Come on in," Suzy said. "You're right on time."

He followed her into the living room where she had a glass of 21-year-old Ben Nevis waiting for him. Doing a bad Jackie Gleason impression, Fin took her hand and pulled her close again.

"Baby, you're the greatest!"

"So, how'd it go?" Suzy asked as they settled together on the sofa.

Fin looked at her and sighed.

"Better than I could have ever hoped."

"Yeah?"

Fin took a sip of the Ben Nevis and savored the burn as it slithered smoothly down his throat.

"The people from Intrepid had no idea what they were in for. They were about to get their heads handed to them by Universal before I stepped in."

"Before you stepped in?" Suzy asked. "You mean you stood up to Universal Studios?" The look of admiration on her face warmed Fin even more than the Scotch.

"I did. Intrepid came up with a damn good screenplay. I didn't want it to go to waste. So, I told Universal that I'd rather sign on with Paramount or Warner Brothers than let this opportunity pass me by.

"Daryl was amazing. He picked up my idea and negotiated a deal where Universal puts up a chunk of capital to coproduce the movie with Intrepid. His deal also said that Universal pays me a million and a half up front, plus four percent of box office."

Suzy gasped, but Fin shrugged.

"Universal countered with *a million* up front and *three* percent of box office. Which we accepted." Fin smiled, his face flushed with excitement. "I expressed my desire for Peter Jackson to produce and direct. I don't know if they'll go with that or not, but . . ."

"Fin," Suzy cooed and snuggled into him. "Look at you being all manly and shit!"

"I am the very model of a masculine grammarian," he replied with an almost English accent.

"Okay, that was impressive," Suzy said.

Fin took another sip, then tilted his head so he could see Suzy's face better.

"How did it go with Michelle?"

Suzy looked up at him somberly and nodded.

"It went well. I mean it was hard, obviously. And, well, as it turned out, her mother killed her."

"What?" Fin leaned forward, alarmed, to look Suzy in the eyes.

"Yeah. And she tried to kill *me*."

"Oh my god!"

"Yeah. Fortunately, Michelle was there, obviously. And her brother showed up. He's the one who really saved me. But it all worked out. She's under arrest and the police are investigating."

"Investigating what?"

"Well, apparently, she also killed at least two of her boyfriends for their money. Michelle was cremated, so that murder can't be proven, unless they can get Joan to confess. The police don't make a practice of taking the word of ghost whisperers."

"Yeah," Fin said, "that sure is a good name. I wish it wasn't already taken."

"I know," Suzy smiled. "Anyway, I don't know about Joe or Paul, Joan's previous boyfriends. The police are looking into it. But at least Nicky, Michelle's brother, was a witness to Joan's attempted murder of me."

"Oh my god," Fin repeated.

"I know. But it's okay, honey. I'm fine. And Michelle is too, now."

They both allowed a few moments of silence to pass in honor of Michelle.

"Damn," Fin finally said, "I go away for a couple of days and look what happens."

"I know," Suzy replied. "Good news, though. You don't have to change your name to Fin Quinn."

"Well, that's good to know."

"Yeah." Suzy paused, looking down at her cup, feeling a little more serious. She looked up at Fin. "My maiden name was Drummond, and I gave it up years ago. Quinn was Mark's name. I guess I've finally accepted that Mark is my past. That time will always be a part of me, but my future is with you.

"And I've decided that, for you, I can endure the annoyance of officially changing my name."

"Suzy MacKinley," Fin said. "I have to admit I like the sound of that." Then, he leaned closer, pressing his lips briefly against her temple. "But seriously, I don't care what your name is, as long as you're with me."

"Mmm, good answer, Mr. Jones."

Afterthoughts and Acknowledgments

Writing is a mostly solitary activity. A writer needs to be inside his own head in order to pull out the story and get it down on the page. That doesn't necessarily mean, however, that he does it all by himself.

Informal consultations of friends, online and otherwise, helped to introduce and solidify ideas in my head and flesh them out for the story. To all those who contributed in that way, thank you!

A big thank-you to Chuck Lovatt who provided invaluable editing insight. I always thought I was pretty good with English. Thanks to you, Chuck, I see that I ain't so good as I thought I wuz. But my hope, now, is that the book will be a more pleasant experience for the reader.

The historical portions of my books usually take place more than a century in the past. Stories set that far back leave a little wiggle room since nobody alive today can comment on the exact feel of a time or situation.

That's not to say that there's no information about such times. Much has been written and, depending on how far back, photos have even been taken, to establish what a particular time or event was like. I do tons of research in order to try to make my stories authentic, not only to the time, but to the characters, as well. Still, its distance from the present often allows for some artistic license.

It's not so easy to fudge things that most people know for certain about the period, because anybody with their memory still intact will remember. To an extent, that even includes me. Certain things like the crash of 2008 still weigh heavily on the minds of a lot of people.

Having my muse and sounding board within easy reach has been a blessing for me. Bouncing ideas off of her, discussing these events from a different point of view, have been invaluable. So Linda, my heartfelt thanks to you for your constant encouragement, support, love and understanding.

Finally, I'd like to thank my readers. Granted, you're not the *reason* I write, but it's nice to have others appreciate the stories that fill my head. It provides a much more logical-sounding rationalization than just clearing out space in my noggin. So I'm glad you're there and interested, and I hope I can continue to provide a little entertainment for you.

If you enjoyed this book, please consider leaving a brief review at Amazon.

www.ingramcontent.com/pod-product-compliance
Lightning Source LLC
Chambersburg PA
CBHW031335170626
46807CB00002B/712